Readers love
RAINE O'TIERNEY

Sweet Giordan, Please Remember

"The scenes were vivid, they were vibrant and they flew off the page and into my heart."

—Boys in Our Books

"O'Tierney is honestly a gifted writer, and she's proven it with Sweet Giordan, Please Remember."

—Prism Book Alliance

Under the Table and Into His Heart

"I needed light, short, and sweet. Under the Table fit the bill perfectly."

—Prism Book Alliance

"The book was downright amazing..."

—MM Good Book Reviews

"Hits the spot for something sweet and yummy."

—The Romance Reviews

MOST BEAUTIFUL
Words

RAINE O'TIERNEY

Dreamspinner Press

Published by
DREAMSPINNER PRESS

5032 Capital Circle SW, Suite 2, PMB# 279, Tallahassee, FL 32305-7886 USA
http://www.dreamspinnerpress.com/

Most Beautiful Words
© 2014 Raine O'Tierney.

Cover Art
© 2014 Brooke Albrecht
http://brookealbrechtstudio.blogspot.com.
Cover content is for illustrative purposes only and any person depicted on the cover is a model.

ISBN: 978-1-63216-210-6
Digital ISBN: 978-1-63216-211-3
Library of Congress Control Number: 2014947607
First Edition October 2014

Printed in the United States of America
ⓧ
This paper meets the requirements of
ANSI/NISO Z39.48-1992 (Permanence of Paper).

This story is dedicated first, and foremost, to my grandfather, a truly amazing man. I would give anything to spend just one more afternoon listening to your stories again, Paw-Paw.

And to Evin, who cried when he read it.

ACKNOWLEDGMENTS

I want to thank Mikhail Shadeed who was the first person to come to me and say, "This is really good." I also could not have made the story what it is without Lisa Campbell's guidance and wisdom.

Thank you to Jes Ford and Erin Davies for your talented edits, and to Jennifer Holsey, Amy Gretenstein, and Lisa Palmer for reading the painfully unedited first draft. I am so lucky to have such amazing women in my life.

AUTHOR'S NOTE

TIME.

When we're young, and sometimes not so young, we think we have forever.

This misconception led to one of my most enduring regrets: I wish I'd spent more time listening to my Paw-Paw's stories.

I try to justify it. I was young, he was old. I was interested in other things. But the regret persists.

We lost him a few years ago to that cruel bastard, Alzheimer's.

I know some of his stories. I know his name wasn't really Sam—but when he played "Sam the Hobo" at school, the nickname stuck. I know a grenade bounced off his chest in Korea. It was a dud. I know there's a little church in Kurten, Texas that he and his father built together. I know he was an exceptional carpenter who measured and re-measured every piece of wood before he made a cut. I know his Daddy was mean. I know the family was poor in a way that I can't even conceptualize "poor." I know he loved all of us with his whole heart.

Still, I wish I knew more.

Part of why Autumn has so much trouble letting go of her Great-Pop in The Most Beautiful Words in the World, is because of her love for his stories. She can't imagine a world where she won't get to hear more.

My Paw-Paw is gone. And I would give anything to listen to him again, even just for one hour. Because I can't, Autumn listens for me.

Stories are meant for sharing. Too many of us take them to our graves. If you're lucky enough to know your family's stories—pass them on! Make them live! Share. And listen when you have the opportunity.

I love you, Paw-Paw. I truly believe you're in your own version of the Valley, making beautiful things with your hands. I have to believe this, because like Autumn, I can't imagine that I won't ever have another chance to listen to you.

—Raine O'Tierney

CHAPTER 1

TOM SQUINTED over the top of his glasses at the two bottles in his hands, trying to remember, as he did every time he made the short trip to the pharmacy, which brand Virginia preferred. She was never the type to yell, and he didn't think she'd even make a fuss, really, but she would give him that look, and he'd know—as he always did—that he'd made a mistake. After almost fifty years of marriage, he knew his wife's looks.

He set one bottle down, the green one with the yellow cap, and tried to imagine it on the bathroom counter. Except this particular brand made lots of pills, and he could see, in his mind, ten bottles with this same design. The pink bottle was familiar, but he felt like he could remember her saying, "Now Tommy, don't buy this one. I don't like the way it makes me feel after I take it." Then again, that could have been a whole different bottle for a whole different pill, or maybe he'd made it all up.

With his free hand, he felt in his pocket for change before he remembered they'd pulled out the payphone outside, leaving a gaping hole in the wall. Hadn't worked half the time anyway. Times like these, Tom wondered if he oughtn't get himself a cell phone; his grandkids had been harping on him about it for long enough.

"Daddy, what if the car breaks down on the side of the road?"

"Do what I've always done," he told them.

"Fix it? Daddy, your hands are shaking so bad these days. And you can't just rely on passersby—they're liable to mug you."

"Nonsense."

"Just let me get you a phone. I'll pay for it. We'll get the simplest one they have on the market."

But that was the thing about getting older; simple wasn't so simple anymore. The kids spoke a foreign language half the time, even when they were talking in English. And their toys and gadgets and electronics, even the "simple" ones, confused him. His great-granddaughter, Hannah, had a phone that looked like a tiny computer, and she carried it everywhere she went. Even to the bathroom. Nah, he didn't need a cell phone. He wouldn't be able to work it. Just another piece of plastic taking up space in his life. Virginia still used her old typewriter when she wanted to write up a letter, so more often than not, their computer sat dead in the office.

Tom shifted uncomfortably, his arthritic knees protesting that he'd been standing too long. He should get the green bottle with the yellow lid, he decided. He had a bad feeling about the other one, and he had no way of knowing which was correct unless he drove home.

He put the bottle up on the checkout counter at the pharmacy, along with a bag of cough drops, menthol rub, and Epsom salts, and waited for the young lady pharmacist to notice him. She was tall and slender with dark brown hair she'd pulled back, except one piece, which was hanging down loose in her face. She would have been pretty, except for her sour expression. And she was ignoring him.

Tom glanced down at the bell and shifted his legs again. He hated to ring it when she was standing right there, but she didn't seem to notice him either. He cleared his throat, and when that did nothing he said, "Excuse me, Miss?"

She shot him a look that said she didn't like being interrupted. Except she hadn't been doing anything that he could see—except ignoring him.

"Floor purchases at the front," she said.

A muscle twitched in his cheek. Time was the pharmacist came out and shook your hand when he made a sale. This little girl—could have been his granddaughter's age—had no service skills.

"I'm picking up a prescription," he told her as calmly as he could manage. His hands were starting to shake, and his knees burned, and he felt a little dizzy. It was hot in the store. He needed to get outside, take in a few cool breaths, and he'd be fine. But he couldn't leave without their prescriptions.

"Name," she prompted him with no apology.

"Johnson," he said, "Thomas and Virginia. Should be four prescriptions between us."

She took an extra-long time getting up and checking the rows and rows of metal shelves for his request. Meanwhile, the room really had started to spin. He had these dizzies sometimes. He'd pay, and he'd sit down, and he'd be fine.

"Here we go," she said after the longest time, and punched the numbers into the register. "Four hundred and fifty-seven thirty."

"Four hundred?" he repeated, flabbergasted.

"Yup," she said, holding out the Y in the word. She cut her eyes over to something or someone behind her.

"Just last month it was three hundred."

"Price went up on the heart meds," she told him, unconcerned.

"A hundred dollars?"

She stared at him.

"Could you possibly check on it? Check to make sure there wasn't an error in the pricing?"

She looked at him and tucked the loose hairs back behind her ear. She examined the bottles and then back at the register and then back at him and said, "Four hundred and fifty-seven thirty."

For a long time after he left the store, Tom sat in his old Dodge and stared at the wheel. The dizzies hadn't passed, even with gulp after gulp of cool air. But his knees were bothering him so badly he couldn't stand, even propped against the brick side of pharmacy. Slowly he laid his head against the ribbed wheel and closed his eyes. Somewhere in the back of his mind, he realized he'd bought the wrong pills for Virginia. It was the pink bottle she wanted, not the yellow and green one.

THE YOUNG police officer just happened to be starting his patrol when he walked past the truck, and he found an elderly man slumped over the wheel. The officer knocked on the window, causing the man to stir. He turned his head slightly, blinked with heavy lids, but there was no light of recognition in his eyes. His mouth worked, opening and closing, and when the officer pulled open the door, he heard the man's gibbering. The old man pressed the gas, but the car didn't move because the keys had fallen out of the ignition.

"—n-needs her pills," he mumbled over and over. The young officer saw the pained look on the man's face, saw the white foam that had leaked from the corners of his mouth and crusted there, saw the way he could barely hold himself up, and the violence with which his hands were shaking.

"Sir?"

The officer grabbed the radio at his hip as the old man reached out for his dashboard where several photographs were taped. There was a picture of a young, redheaded girl with wide, curious green eyes. The officer requested an ambulance just as the man slumped off the steering wheel, his hand catching, and tearing loose, the photograph of the girl. It fluttered to the floorboard, and he landed in the passenger seat.

CHAPTER 2

AUTUMN SAT rigid in the stiff orange hospital chair, gripping the edge of her pretty skirt with pale hands. She forced herself not to look at Mama, who was pretending she wasn't crying. Every once in a while, Mama's throat became too tight or her nose too stuffy to draw a breath, and she let out a little gasping sob. Autumn wanted to reach out and touch her mother and comfort her, but every time she tried, Mama just cried harder, bending over until she couldn't breathe. Autumn felt helpless, and she kept her fingers knotted in her skirt.

Across a small aisle, sitting in the other set of joined, uncomfortable chairs, Aunt Janie talked quietly to her new husband. Her aunt's eyes looked tired, like she'd stayed up late reading a sad book, but she wasn't crying. Autumn's cousin, Hannah, sat next to her mother, slumped all the way forward, texting furiously between her legs. Her hair—bleached bright blonde and straightened—blocked most of her face. All Autumn could see was a slice of pimply cheek caked with makeup. She definitely wasn't crying. Every once in a while Hannah would look up at her mother and whine, "I'm bored. Can we go home yet?"

Even though she was twelve and all her friends did, Autumn tried not to curse. Her best friend, Emma, was a wordsmith when it came to bad language. She would have said Hannah was a bitch and a half.

Hannah didn't care that Great-Pop was in the ICU. She didn't care that everyone else was worried. She didn't care that Autumn's mother was crying or that Autumn felt like her heart might break into a million little shards. She definitely didn't care that Autumn was right on the edge of puking. Her stomach was nervous all the time anyway, and now? Now it was like a zombie eating itself.

Hannah sat back slightly and, flipping her phone around, took a photo of herself making a kissy-face at the camera. Then she went back to texting.

"I hate you," Autumn muttered under her breath, and for a minute she wished it was Hannah in the ICU and not Great-Pop. Then she remembered every book she'd ever read about getting what you wish for, and she flushed to her ears and silently took it all back. She wished *none* of them were in the hospital. She wished she was at home, doing her geography homework, listening to Vanity's new album, and talking to Emma on the phone. She wanted everyone she cared about to be happy and healthy. She wanted to go over to Great-Pop's tomorrow and have him tell her a story or play a tree-guessing game with her. She wanted him to snooze in his big armchair while his two dachshunds, Oscar and Rudy, vied to be king of his lap.

Mama's phone rang in her purse, startling them both. She grappled with the zipper and tossed things to Autumn as she dug. Three red lipsticks, a hairbrush so full of her hair that the bristles barely showed through the top, her bulging wallet, a rubber-banded package of peanuts, a bottle of perfume, the big set of keys, the little set of keys, and then her day planner all went into Autumn's lap. She'd just pulled out the *Weekly Horoscope* mini-book she'd bought from the gas station when she found the phone.

"H-Hello?" she answered in a shaking voice. "Oh, Terri, where are you? Are you with Mom? Okay.... Yes.... No, we haven't heard anything more yet. No. No. They wouldn't even let Grandmomma in yet. Yeah, Amy Jo took her home."

Autumn had only seen Great-Mom for a moment while Aunt Amy Jo talked with the doctor. She looked very small and frail, and she kept glancing down the hall, as if she could somehow see right through the walls to where Great-Pop lay in his bed. Great-Mom didn't cry, but her face was china-white and tight, and Autumn thought that at any moment she might crack. Autumn felt like she should have gone to her and told her it would be okay. She should have maybe hugged her or something. But Great-Mom was strangely quiet at the best of times, and even though Autumn had known her for twelve full years, she never knew what to say to her.

"I wish he'd just get it over with," Hannah muttered from across the aisle. Her thumbs worked furiously. Either Aunt Janie didn't hear her, or she was so used to her daughter's snarkiness that she just ignored it. Autumn heard though, and she looked up at her cousin.

"Get *what* over with?" she asked, quietly but firmly.

Hannah half smirked at her, eyes narrowing, sarcasm painting her face like her caked-on foundation. Then she rearranged her expression and looked innocent and confused.

"What, Autumn?" she sneered in a mockingly sugary voice.

"You said—" Autumn spoke loud enough that every member of the family within earshot could hear her. "—That you wished he'd just 'get it over with.' What do you want him to get over with?"

"I don't know what you're talking about," Hannah lied, and looked at her as if she was crazy.

Aunt Janie, unable to ignore them as Autumn's volume continued to rise, broke away from her conversation. "Something wrong, honey?"

She could feel the heat in her face, and Autumn spluttered, "Hannah just said she wishes he'd 'get it over with.'" The more she repeated the words, the angrier she got. "She said she wishes Great-Pop would…." Faced with saying it out loud—that her vile cousin actually *wished* their Great-Pop, one of Autumn's most favorite people in the whole world, would just die—her courage failed her completely and she dropped her head. "Nothing. Never mind," she said in a tiny, defeated voice.

Hannah waited only until her mother had turned away before sneering under her breath, "Tattletale slutbaby."

"All right, well, we'll see you when you can get here," her mother said as she hung up the phone. Autumn shifted uncomfortably and chanced a glance at her mother. The phone conversation, for the moment, seemed to have stilled her tears. It was as if she were seeing Autumn for the first time that day.

"Gosh, baby-doll, we didn't even stop to get you a change of clothes."

Autumn looked down at her neat skirt, now wrinkled in her sweaty hands. It was Honor Roll day and she'd dressed in her nicest clothes, though they were a little small and a lot uncomfortable. Her mother had curled her hair and sprayed it that morning when everything seemed perfectly normal and she thought she'd be eating pizza in the principal's office with the other three students who'd also made Honor Roll. But at 10:34, when they were having DEAR—Drop Everything and Read—in English, the principal's secretary came on the intercom and told her to report to the office.

When Autumn heard the announcement, she was embarrassed and excited and worried all at once. She'd never been called to the office before, and as she stood, the other kids in her class all "Oooooood" as if she'd done something totally illicit. Her teacher hushed them with rolled eyes. Autumn had been an Ooo'er in the past; being on the receiving end of it, she didn't think she'd do it to the next kid who had their name called over the intercom.

All the way down the large, deserted hallway, brightly decorated in the school's colors of yellow and black for the Fighting Bees, Autumn wondered what she'd done to warrant this privilege or… punishment? And about the time she reached the office with its glass walls and its two secretaries, Mrs. Anderson—the nice one—and Miss Dyer—the mean one, her nervous stomach was turning somersaults. She hadn't done *anything*; she was sure of it. Autumn was the good one. Autumn made it to class on time, she didn't curse, she raised her hand and answered questions; she studied. She was sort of a teacher's pet, even. Unless they had found out about her and Hunter kissing on a dare underneath the far basketball goal? But there was no way they'd send her to the principal's office for that, right?

She could hardly breathe as she looked for Mrs. Anderson. Instead, she found Mama standing near the desk with Miss Dyer. Her mother's eyes were red, and tear streaks cut into her makeup.

"Autumn, honey, something bad has happened," she explained, holding her arms out. Autumn instinctively threw herself into her mother's embrace and began to cry because Mama was.

On the drive to the hospital, Mama told her Great-Pop had had a stroke, and it didn't look good.

"But they can fix him, right?" Autumn asked.

"Maybe," Mama said, but tears crested and broke as she did. Autumn didn't push her.

CHAPTER 3

TWO YEARS ago, Autumn had had a high tea to celebrate her tenth birthday. She got the idea from *Pretty* magazine. There was an article about her favorite singer, Vanity, who invited all her famous friends over for a high tea to celebrate her sweet sixteen. They had pictures of Vanity laughing and winking as she held up her teacup, and a 10-step process for hosting "A Kick-A B-Day, High Society Style." Autumn's best friend Emma was on board immediately.

"I get to wear a boa, right?" she asked.

"Well…." No one in the photographs had a boa, but Emma insisted. Together they decided on decorations and finalized the guest list. Emma made the invitations. At the bottom she wrote, *Autumn is registered through the fabulous Emma. Please consult with her before making your gift selection.*

"I'm registered with you?" Autumn asked.

"Trust me, you want it this way. You think Vanity doesn't have someone yes and no her gifts? This way you won't get crap."

Since she was turning double digits, Autumn's mother took her shopping, and she got a brand-new dress from the department store. It didn't really look like Vanity's, but it was the same color—hot pink. She wore gloves and a glittering fake tiara that Mama helped her fix in her hair. And even though she wasn't normally allowed to wear makeup (except on Halloween), Mama put a little powder on her and a smear of eye shadow and lipstick. Emma came over early to help her greet her guests, which was really her way of letting them know that *she* was the best friend. Except for one point where Lisa and Jes got into an argument over a book they'd both read, it was the best birthday party Autumn ever had.

That night, she and Mama went over to eat dinner at Great-Mom and Great-Pop's. A bunch of her aunts and uncles and her grandmother were there too. It wasn't meant to be a celebration for Autumn; no one had even said happy birthday, actually. It just so happened that her birthday was on the same day as her great-grandparents' wedding anniversary, and they liked to celebrate every year by spending time with their family.

Autumn knew she was sort of weird. For one thing, not a lot of the kids had their great-grandparents anymore, and the ones who did, didn't spend a whole lot of time with them. They were old. Kids had better things to do than hang out with old people. But those kids didn't have Tommy Johnson for their Great-Pop. If it were up to Autumn, she'd have spent every single Friday evening over at her great-grandparents' house listening to Great-Pop tell her a story.

When she and her mother finally got close enough to give Great-Pop and Great-Mom their hugs and kisses, Great-Pop whispered in her ear, "Happy birthday, princess."

"Thank you." She smiled prettily at him, pleased to her core that someone had remembered.

"The big one-oh."

"Yup!" She grinned.

"I guess you're a little old for me to push you on the swing now, huh?"

Autumn thought about this. He hadn't pushed her since she was a little kid, and now that she was a mature woman of ten, she was *embarrassingly* too old for it. But if they went out to swing, Great-Pop might tell her one of his secret stories, a story no one else had ever heard.

"Well, *I* could swing and you could come... hang out with me." She paused on "hang out." Now that she was ten, she had to say things like that, because if she said "play," she'd sound like a baby. Like on the bus one afternoon, she had made the mistake of asking Emma if she wanted to come over and play. Well, the boys in the seat in front of them started to make fun until Emma threatened to punch them. Autumn learned her lesson.

Great-Mom smiled at something her daughter, Autumn's grandmother, said, and thanked her for all the lovely decorations.

"But I don't want you to miss your party, Great-Pop."

"How long do you plan on swinging? All night?" he teased her, and she giggled. Then he announced to the room that he was going to go outside with his birthday princess for a little while, and that he would be back in time to eat cake. It made her feel good because after he said that, everyone told her happy birthday, even Uncle Denny. His was the most boisterous, and she had to dodge his arms when he reached out for her. He smelled like Daddy's beer, and when Denny had been drinking, he would tickle her until she couldn't breathe.

Outside, when she was settled on the swing, Great-Pop asked her with a thoughtful smile, "So what would you like to hear about?"

There was no question about it—she wanted to hear something totally and completely brand-new. She begged, "Tell me something no one in the whole wide world knows!"

For a long time, Great-Pop was quiet. Then he said, "Something no one else knows, huh?"

She began to swing, legs forward, legs back, pumping herself higher and higher. So he *did* have a secret! Autumn loved secrets. She and Emma had started a secret club this year. Before that day, it was just called the Emma and Autumn Club, but now that they were both ten, on Monday they would start calling it the Emma and Autumn Double-Digits Club. There was a diary they traded back and forth between classes that had a little lock on it. Each of them had a key they wore around their necks. In the diary they exchanged secret messages—mostly about boys they thought were cute and how annoying their teacher was and what they overheard the other girls saying in the bathroom.

For a long time the only sound was the whoosh of the pink crepe material of her dress as she rose higher and higher in the air. Concerned she had upset him somehow, Autumn leaned her head backward, her gem-flower tiara slipping into the topknot Mama had fixed up. He didn't look mad, just a little distant, like he'd gone somewhere else.

"You don't have to," she said, disappointed. Over the years, Great-Pop had told her many stories about his life: places he'd visited, stories about his children and grandchildren and great-grandchildren and treasured memories of his childhood. But maybe he wasn't ready to share this one. Maybe he'd changed his mind about letting her in on his secret.

"I think it's time I told you my very favorite story," he said, slow and deliberate. Some of the age ebbed from his voice as he did.

"Really?" she asked, excitement welling again. With each and every story he told, she had asked, *Is this one your favorite?* And he would always say no. No, he was saving his favorite for another day. That he was finally ready to tell her his favorite story made her feel special and loved.

"Tell me," she insisted earnestly.

"Give me a minute, princess. Unveiling a secret you've kept so long…. Well, it's not easy."

Autumn considered herself an excellent secret keeper. She hadn't told anyone about Emma's crush on Matthew Wright, and she hadn't told anyone that Mama and Daddy were fighting again. She never even told anyone that it was Beth who pulled the fire alarm so they could all get out of their science test.

"I capital S Swear," Autumn said, even though Mama told her never to swear, "that I will not tell anyone your secret."

Great-Pop looked through the window to where Great-Mom was smiling with her daughters for a photo and, clearing his throat, he asked very quietly, "Do you, uh, know any kids in your class that have…." He cleared his throat again, harder this time. "Two mothers or two fathers?"

"Any kids with gay parents?" Autumn asked, thinking nothing of it. Skylar M, who had almost the exact same schedule as her this year, had two fathers. And when she was in third grade, the Biggs brothers' mom had a girlfriend, but Autumn thought she was married to a man now. Even her favorite actor of *all time*, Joey Sullivan, had two moms. He had brought both of them to the *Kids TV Awards*. "Yeah," she said. "Of course. Why?"

Great-Pop shook his head and smiled to himself. "It's a different world."

"Why are you asking about gay people, Great-Pop?" she wondered, swinging higher and higher. She reached out her feet and tried to kick a low-hanging branch. It was just out of her reach.

"When I was a young man, I was… in love with…."

She figured it out before he actually said it, just because he'd been asking about gay parents. She cut him off before he could speak.

"If you were in love with a boy, Great-Pop, then why did you marry Great-Mom?"

"Because I lost him. He died."

"Is this a story about losing him?" She didn't think she wanted to hear about that. Even if it was a secret. Even if the story had never been told. It wasn't a day for sad stories. It was her birthday, and it was Great-Pop's anniversary.

"No," he said. "You wanted a story I never told anyone. Well, this is it. It's a story about friendship."

"I thought he was your love?"

"All good loves start out as friendships, princess," Great-Pop said, his hands warm and firm on her back. "Do you want to hear?"

Oh how she wanted to hear. More than anything she'd ever wanted before. Autumn nodded quickly.

"I noticed him at church first."

Autumn looked around the yard. The sun was burning out of the sky, leaving a swath of sunset colors in its wake, and near the edges of the yard where the juniper bushes grew, tiny bursts of green illuminated the growing darkness as the fireflies came out to dance.

"He kept his hair long, which wasn't the style at the time."

She thought again about Joey Sullivan on *That Rocks!* It was the best show on television, and all the girls in her grade thought Joey was the cutest. Of course he was her favorite too. He had a really great smile with a dimple and really long hair, almost as long as hers. He tied it back in a ponytail.

"And he dressed really casual for Sunday service. My step-momma—your great-great-grandmother—used to say that his family was poor trash and that the bank ought to do us all a favor and take those acres of dust they called a farm and drive them out of town. Step-Momma was a snob, and we were poor too. But we weren't poor like the McMillans, and that made her think she was better than them."

It was the first time she'd ever heard him say anything about his stepmother. She decided anyone that had anything bad to say about the young man her Great-Pop loved wasn't a good person, and she immediately disliked the great-great-grandmother she'd never known.

"What did he look like, Great-Pop?"

"Handsome. Mischievous."

"What color was his hair?"

"Brown."

"And long," she repeated for herself. Joey Sullivan had blond hair, so she had to adjust for that.

"With bright blue eyes."

She fixed that too.

"So you talked to him at church?" she spurred him anxiously. She wanted more!

Great-Pop moved quietly over to the rust-stained iron chair next to the bushes. "I met him at the little library. The librarian there was an old maid named Miss Palmer, and she was *mean*...."

CHAPTER 4

TOMMY JOHNSON was no sneak, but that day, for no good reason except he wanted to, he was slinking around corners and following someone like a secret agent in one of his favorite spy stories. He'd caught a glimpse of his target in the drugstore buying a soda and headache powders. Normally Tommy would have just walked on by, but today he stopped, and waited, and watched the young man cross the street.

Tommy knew who he was, of course. Everyone had seen him in church, even though he and his momma never stayed for the potlucks or came to the cakewalks. He attended service wearing slacks and suspenders over a shirt with rolled sleeves, but no suit coat. And his hair hung over his ears. Not enough for the minister to turn him out in the street (because Pastor Friday was a kind and patient old man) but enough to be inappropriate. When he smiled, and he was always smiling—or smirking, rather—during service, he looked rakish.

Tommy wondered, running his fingers through his own short curls, if he would look as attractive as Roy if he had longer hair. The McMillan boy was an odd one in a community that prided itself on sameness, and Tommy couldn't stop staring.

Past Murphy's Dress Shop and Peggy's, the hair salon Aunt Margaret ran, Roy turned the corner, and Tommy had to hurry down the walk to keep up with him. Tommy wasn't an exceptionally good spy. He made it to the corner just in time to see Roy pat a pair of school children on the head as they left the little library carrying their books. Then he slipped through the door.

The library?

Tommy hadn't been in the library since he was a young boy, though he still kept his library card in his wallet behind his license and draft card. Hesitating for only a moment on the worn copper door handle, Tommy steeled his resolve and followed Roy inside the musty, one-room building.

Miss Palmer, the same librarian who'd worked the Campbell Springs Library since the dawn of time, glared suspiciously at him from behind her glasses and raised a finger to her lips in warning, even though he hadn't made a peep. As small as the library was—one could lean over past the first shelf and see all the way to the back wall—it sure was crammed full of books. The rows of shelving were so close he had to turn completely to the side and scoot along toward the next open space. A fatter man, like the town's ruddy-faced banker, would definitely have gotten stuck. Tommy stifled a chuckle as he imagined it. He could see Miss Palmer readying her finger again.

Along the back wall, which was covered with local maps, individual class portraits from the last twenty years, and a framed photograph of the president, there sat a single study desk and a rickety old table with two equally rickety old chairs. A chess board sat on top of the table, its pieces already set to go. Roy was in the corner, facing Tommy, holding one of the pieces while studying the board.

Silently, Tommy sat down across from Roy McMillan.

Tommy's pieces were made of blond wood; his opponent's, mahogany. Tommy looked over at the other young man and waited for him to say something, but Roy just smiled that rakish smile and made his move. Tommy pretended to think for a long while. In truth, he didn't know chess at all. He knew the names of some of the pieces—his king and queen; the little ones were pawns. He wasn't sure about the others. And he wasn't sure how they moved. But since it was on a checkers board, he decided he would slide a pawn like checkers, moving it one diagonal space and then looking up.

Roy continued to smile, his bright blue eyes mischievous. He moved one of his pieces—one of the ones Tommy didn't know, a horse maybe?—in a really weird way. Tommy watched the move uncertainly, not knowing if it was legal. For a while, Tommy continued to move his pawns like checkers, but after Roy had zagged all over the board, Tommy decided he would too. He took his little pawn and moved it in the same L-shape he'd seen Roy use. The pawn landed on a space occupied by his opponent's piece. He knocked it over.

"Got that one."

"Guess you did," Roy said, his voice deep. He seemed bemused. Roy took the piece off the board and made a different move. Tommy moved again, knocking another over. Again, he removed it. And so it went with Tommy making wild moves he did not understand, and the other removing pieces and setting them to the side until all that was left of the mahogany pieces was one little tower.

"Checkmate," Tommy told him, because he'd heard it somewhere before.

Roy smiled and ran his finger down the smooth side of the tower.

The game wasn't really that hard; a lot like some kind of crazy checkers actually, if Tommy understood it. And he didn't think he'd done anything illegal, or else Roy would have called him on it.

"I just have to get that tower from you and then I've won it, right?"

"Right."

"Okay," Tommy said, and moved his queen, who had been a fierce piece the whole game, across the board and knocked the tower over. "I'm Tommy Johnson, by the way."

"Roy McMillan."

"I've got a secret for you, Roy. I don't actually know much about chess."

"Really?" Roy drew the word out. "Well, I couldn't tell."

Tommy didn't know if he was being sarcastic or not, but his smile seemed friendly enough. "I've seen you in church."

From behind the cramped rows of books, Miss Palmer let out a long and wet sounding "Shh!" and, given that they were the only two occupants of the library, she must have been aiming it at them. Tommy choked down a laugh. She sounded like a mean old snake. He dropped his voice, which had been reaching audible levels before, down to practically nothing. "I've seen you in church," he repeated.

"I've seen you too." Somehow when Roy said it, it sounded less friendly and more…?

"I followed you here from the drugstore," Tommy whispered.

"I know."

He tried not to flush.

"Don't you want to know why?"

Roy shrugged and said, "Sure. Why?"

For a second Tommy didn't quite know what to say, which was weird considering he'd spurred the other to ask. He guessed he wanted to know more about the young man he saw at service every Sunday.

Their church was a little, white-painted, one-room chapel with windows made of dark, stained glass. Tommy's grandfather had built it, and Tommy had helped when he was just a boy, hauling nails and paint up the ladder all day—sometimes drinking water and food, too. He was proud of his church. It was a good place where good people went. And some of the congregation didn't think that Roy McMillan was a very good person, but why? Because he didn't dress right? Because his hair was long? Did that make him bad?

Roy sang along with the hymns every Sunday. Didn't even need to open the hymnal; he knew all the songs by heart. He stood when the congregation stood, sat when they sat. He took communion. But he smirked a lot. And he didn't look at Pastor Friday when he gave the sermon.

"Did you hear yesterday's sermon?" Tommy asked.

He knew why he'd followed, and it wasn't to ask about the sermon. He'd followed because Roy McMillan *distracted* him when he was trying to commune with the Lord, and he wanted to know why.

Roy nodded. "Sure did. Need a refresher? It was all fire and brimstone."

Tommy grinned. "He read from Psalms."

"Oh." Roy shrugged. "Guess I heard something else."

Yes, Roy was definitely distracting.

"You want to go somewhere where we can talk out loud?"

"I would like that a lot, Tommy Johnson."

And they stood, Tommy careful not to let his chair scrape across the floor. Roy was less cautious. Another angry "Shh!" cut across the small space.

WHEN MISS Palmer made rounds through her library that evening, straightening books and tidying up that sacred space, she would notice, with both horror and full affront, that her chessboard was missing a single piece—a dark mahogany rook.

CHAPTER 5

HIS EYES slowly cracked open and he found himself in an unfamiliar room, in an unfamiliar world, in an unfamiliar body.

He could name everything he saw. He understood he was in a four-poster bed with a patchwork quilt tucked up around his body and that if he turned his head, he could see an oak dresser with a vanity mirror and a stone water basin. Nouns and adjectives were no problem for him. The problem instead was that even though he knew what they were called, he couldn't remember ever, in his whole existence, seeing any other object with the same name. For that matter, he wasn't exactly sure of his whole existence, either.

When he sat up, the reflection in the cracked and fogged mirror sat up with him. When he raised his hand, the reflection did the same, and so he took it on good faith that this was his visage. Those were his dark brown eyes with flecks of gold in them and his tangle of golden curls. He was young; he was male; he was fit; he was relatively good-looking.

He had no concept of self beyond his immediate senses, past what he saw in the mirror. He couldn't recall a single detail about his history or his interests or… anything. But instead of being distressed, he simply decided that since he didn't know who he'd been, he could create who he was. And so he started by naming himself.

"Toren." He spoke aloud.

The name came from nowhere—but he liked the heft of it and the sound of it in the air. He was Toren, and, he decided, this room was his room, and this house was his house. He already liked it a lot, so if it turned out to be true, then he was set. And, if he discovered later that it was actually someone else's house, he could always just redefine himself as a man without a past. That meant he might have to go looking for a home in the future, but it also meant that, for the moment, he was quite secure.

Outside his window, the sky was a vibrant burnt orange, and it bathed the room in sleek golden hues. It was a fine sunset, a very peaceful view, and it gave him the sense that—even though he'd just awoken—it had been a good and productive day. This, he decided, was truth as well.

Only stopping to change into clothes which fit like they were his, Toren took to exploring his new-old home. He walked into each room without knocking and opened drawers and moved papers and looked behind bookshelves. There were many spacious rooms on the upper floor, each cozily furnished in different color schemes. He had been using the brown room, with brown curtains, brown sheets, and brown furniture. The room at the end of the hall was green, and all the accents, the paintings, the pillows, the rugs even—were green. The windowsill overflowed with a row of plants that had grown large under someone's dutiful green thumb.

The only thing that united the rooms was their doors. Plain, simple wooden doors that had ornately fashioned knobs and keyholes— none of them locked.

"I think I'll keep the brown room," he said aloud, having found no other room he liked quite as much as that one. Hearing himself for the second time, he decided he had a good, strong voice.

There were weird rooms that were fun to visit too. There was a room with nothing but wardrobes along every wall, a sewing machine with bolts of cloth, and dressmakers' dummies in various states of dress and undress. And at the very end of the hallway, almost as an afterthought, there was a tiny little room facing south. In it, there was a child-sized bed and smaller furniture, but surely no child would be interested in that space. It was dusty and cobwebbed, and everything in the room was old and shabby. Toren wasn't quite sure what to make of it and thought he could repurpose the room for something better.

The last room upstairs was a small library, stacked floor to ceiling with books, an old table and chessboard with a piece missing, and a writing desk. Perhaps he could move out the furniture from the child's bedroom and replace it with overflow from the library. He could make himself a quiet and comfortable little study that way.

"Later," he said, "too much to explore now."

He took the stairs two at a time and found himself in a spacious sitting room. There were chairs around the fireplace as if the space had been readied for a companionable chat. Through a dining room, he found what was instantly his favorite room of the house, even more so than his bedroom. The kitchen! It smelled just like baking bread, even though the brick oven was cold. He must have a housekeeper or be a rather good hand with a broom, because while the furnishings of his large cottage were a little shabby, everything was spotless. He couldn't imagine a more perfect place to wake up for the first time.

When Toren saw the cheese and freshly baked bread and wine sitting out on the counter, his stomach rumbled, and he felt ravenous hunger.

"I wish you'd show yourself, housekeeper," Toren mused quietly, trying to decide how best to prepare the meal. In the end, he did nothing with the food, save putting it on a plate. Even minimal effort would have resulted in a better meal—but hunger got the best of him and he could only think of sating the craving. He let each bite linger on his tongue. He anticipated the delicious flavors as if he had never tasted anything before.

The wine was sweet and heady, and while he ate he watched the burning sky which had, thankfully, stayed illuminated throughout his meal. He knew he should draw water and rinse his plate and his glass, but while he was keenly interested to see his well or his water pump, he found he had little desire to do the dishes. He decided that he *must* have a housekeeper, because he wasn't a tidy sort of person at all.

Leaving his mess behind for someone else, Toren went out into the blissfully warm evening.

Then he saw her. A figure, hunched nearby, digging in the dirt. His housekeeper? No, he didn't think so. He moved nearer. He didn't think she was the owner of the house, either.

"Hello?" he called out to her, and she lifted her head. He realized he could see the thick carpet of light green ivy that covered the outside of his cottage *through* her translucent face. When she moved, little gold flakes of dust trailed behind her. She was wearing a bandana over her graying curls and she held a trowel in one hand. "Are you...?" When he touched her shoulder, she immediately became solid and she smiled at him—two pearls shy of a wide, toothy grin.

"Ah, Master," she said, "I was waiting for you."

"Were you?" he asked.

"Yes," she agreed with a nod, "You'll be wanting me to plant turnips, I think?"

Did he? He didn't know. He drew his hand back from her and she remained solid, but when he looked away, his mind momentarily on turnips, and then turned back, she had lost all form. She was translucent again, her attention back to the ground where she was digging.

"Turnips will be nice," he said, but she didn't respond.

Toren thought maybe she wasn't real. This didn't frighten him nor did it confuse him.

"Gardener?" he asked, addressing her. She was almost like a placeholder for where a real person would be. He touched her arm again, and again she was made solid.

"Turnips," he repeated, and she nodded.

Several times he did this, turning her real, then making her shimmer away to gold-dust by ignoring her, and never once did she seem bothered or even cognizant of the fact that she was really just scenery. Just part of this place.

"So sad," he said. He did not think he would like to be nothing but dust.

Toren left her to her task and followed the path around the back to a garden bursting with vivid flowers. It was at once chaotic and perfectly maintained. There were deep bushes with clever little hidden entrances. A child or an animal could sneak inside and hide or play. It made him want to get to his knees and try, but he was much too big. Near the back fence, there were raspberry, blueberry, and blackberry bushes around a large oak tree with a rope swing expertly hung. He sat on that swing for a while and considered his world, which was still illuminated in the brightest golden sunset despite the fact that an hour or more must have passed.

Eventually wanderlust and the sense that he was being idle prompted him to go look for the well, which he found past the low stone wall. The ground around the well was mossy, and on a whim he slipped off his shoes and buried his toes into the rich green carpet. It was almost like putting his toes into water. Perfectly pleasant. Leaning over the side of the well, he dropped pebbles into the water below and looked up farther into the woods past his property line. It was late, and if he started now, it would likely be dark before he found anything of interest. He was liable to get lost.

Toren looked back at his cottage, bathed in that strange light.

Would it grow dark?

It was an unusual thought. The sun was made to rise and set. And yet, there it hung, and there it had been hanging as long as he'd been awake. Why wasn't it dark already?

Toren continued to stare into the golden light.

The sun should not dangle in the sky like this, leaving the world aglow for longer than its time.

He decided to wait just a while longer, an hour or more, to see if the sky changed. If it didn't, and if he did not find anything else around the property that caught his immediate interest, he would go into the woods and explore. He hoped to find no one and everything out there.

CHAPTER 6

AUTUMN STIRRED against her mother's arm, slowly opening her eyes. A little bleary and embarrassed, she ran her fingers over her mouth and swiped away a thin line of drool. Hannah and her family were gone, and Autumn was grateful not to be caught drooling. She shifted away from the warmth of Mama's body and cleared her head, wondering how long she'd been asleep. The fluorescent lights and windowless waiting room made it impossible to tell how long she'd been out.

"Did I wake you up?" Mama asked quietly, brushing a strand of hairspray crusted hair out of her face. "We need to get you a shower, baby-doll."

"What time is it? Where did Aunt Janie go?"

"Late. And home," Mama said. "Everyone went home."

"Great-Pop isn't...!" she exclaimed, demanding more than questioning. Her mother gently patted her cheek and encouraged her to lay her head back down.

"No, he isn't. They still aren't letting anyone in to see him. Aunt Terri is tied up, and the others will get here tomorrow. I'm going to wait here tonight and call the family when we have news. Do you want to go home?"

"No." She shook her head, trying to work her skinny fingers through her hair. They caught halfway and stuck. "Where's Grandma?"

"At home with Great-Mom."

"Why isn't Great-Mom here?"

"She's resting."

"When is she coming back?"

"Tomorrow maybe, if she can."

"But he needs her," Autumn argued, refusing to rest her head even for a minute. "He needs her to be with him."

"Shh, baby-doll, I know. But Great-Mom is very old, and she gets weak sometimes. These chairs are too hard on her."

Autumn couldn't believe it. Hard chairs? That was a lame excuse for not being at the hospital with your husband. What kind of wife was she anyway?

"Then he needs *me*," she insisted, which was what she'd really wanted to say from the beginning. There were people everywhere, but none she recognized. Families talking together, couples, and single solitary figures, waiting. The waiting united them. Whether they were texting, typing on their laptops, watching the muted television, or just staring at their locked hands, each of them was waiting for someone. Some stifled—or didn't—their tears. There were few smiles in the waiting room, only those from a family Autumn suspected was waiting for a new baby to come. She wished her family was there for a baby.

"He needs me right beside him. If I could sit with him and talk to him, then he would wake up."

"Shh, Autumn, you're getting loud."

Just then her stomach gurgled so forcefully that even her mother could hear it, and she slapped her hands over her belly. She looked down. She was hungry, but she was also queasy, and that made her afraid to eat. When she was really upset, she always wound up throwing up on herself. It happened at home, it happened at Emma's, and a couple of times it had happened at school. She hoped her mother would ignore it—she always tried to make her eat.

"We should get you something."

"I'm fine," Autumn said. "I just want to wait here for Great-Pop."

"You can't not eat," her mother argued, a touch frustrated.

"I'm not hungry. I'm just going to wait."

"Autumn." Her mother's heavy chest rose and fell with a deep, controlling breath. When she spoke, her voice was quiet but edged with frustration. "Please don't make me take you to your father's."

Autumn instantly and with some horror weighed her options. She knew if her mother forced her to eat, she was going to throw up. But if she did not at least pretend like she would try, then she would be taken away from the warm, if uncomfortable, hospital waiting room and dumped on her father. He didn't care about Great-Pop, and he didn't care about Autumn—even with visitation rights, he never wanted to see her. Besides, she felt like if she could just stay close to him, Great-Pop would get better.

She wished she could crawl into his bed and cuddle up next to him and ask for another story about Roy.

"Can I just have an apple?" she finally asked, and her mother uncurled herself from the chair. She stretched her limbs and groaned as she stood, having sat for way too long. "I'll wait here," Autumn insisted.

When her mother had gone to find an apple for Autumn and a coffee for herself, Autumn took off her heeled shoes and hid her feet up underneath her bottom, pulling her skirt down over her knees. And then she let herself cry, just a little and silently, into her hands. She wanted to sit with Great-Pop and hold his hand. And if he couldn't tell her a story, she'd tell one to him.

Once—no sound escaped her lips as she formed the words—Great-Pop, you and Roy were doing archery in the woods on the neighbor's land, real far down near the creek where no one else ever went. Autumn found that as she thought the words her tears started to dry. She concentrated on forming the words like a prayer, and offered them up to Great-Pop and God and Jesus and anyone who could help her now. The challenge was to see who could shoot the straightest, and Roy was winning.

"YOU'RE GOING to fall!" Roy taunted from the ground below, bow slung over his back.

"You'll just have to catch me!" Tommy called back. Then realizing that made him sound like a little girl, he scoffed, "But it ain't gonna happen, because I've been climbing these trees my whole life."

They were on the Clarks' land, way on the edge of their property, where it became unincorporated. For all he knew, they'd stepped off the Clarks' and were in the middle of nowhere, land owned by no man. Land they could stake claim on for themselves. Either way, no one ever came back here. It wasn't good for much but running and exploring and a little creek fishing, all of which he and his brother, Abner, had done when they were kids. Now he and Roy were showing off for each other—shooting arrows. No really good reason for it; they were probably too old for dumb games like this, but Roy had caught him coming home from work and asked if he wanted to engage in a little friendly competition.

They were wagering something, but Roy hadn't said what. Only that there was a prize for the winner, and Tommy better try his hardest if he wanted to win.

Tommy *was* trying his hardest, but Roy was still winning. Roy not only hit the target dead-on, but he also then shot Tommy's arrow out of the second ring with his own. Tommy was so mad he aimed his bow up in the tree and let an arrow fly.

"That's gonna count as your shot 'less you go up there and get it," Roy told him smugly. So, cursing, Tommy started to climb. Roy was at the base of the tree, throwing his weight into the trunk. It didn't give much, just enough to sway Tommy, who held on easily.

"You want me to fall?" he demanded.

"I want to catch you!" Roy teased back.

He'd found the arrow, the tip barely lodged into the bark overhead. It was just out of his reach, but it seemed loose enough that if he could grab a twig or something, he could knock it free and catch it. Well, there wasn't anything for it; he sure as hell wasn't going to let Roy McMillan win this—not with some unknown prize at stake.

He was reaching out for a slender branch to break off when he saw the butterfly, flexing its gossamer wings in the fading light. Its tiny antennae quivered in the gentle evening breeze. It was a real pretty color—like the royal purple in his sister's crayon box. She might like it, Ardeth, if he caught it for her. If only he had his net.

"Giving you ten seconds there, Tommy!" Roy warned.

"Stuff it—I'll get the damned arrow, I just want to grab this—"

Once again, Roy shook the tree, this time with both his arms and all his might. The butterfly lifted off, escaping Tommy's outstretched fingers by not more than an inch. Worse still, the arrow fell past him, right into Roy's outstretched arms.

"That counts as your hit. Way off target, Tommy. Minus a million points."

Tommy let out a swear that sent birds flying into the air, squawking in protest.

"You're cheating!" he bellowed down below.

"I want to win," Roy told him smugly as Tommy slid down the rough trunk of the tree and landed in the moss at the bottom. It was a stupid thing to get riled about, but he couldn't help it. Roy had done it on purpose. If only he hadn't stopped to try to grab that damned bug.

"You're a fink," he told him sourly.

"You're just a sore loser." Roy shrugged, tossing the arrow aside. "But I'm a good winner, Tommy Johnson. I'll let you have the prize instead of me."

"*Let me*," Tommy muttered. "Since you stole what you know was going to be my win, I'd say you *owe* me the prize."

"Keep on thinkin' those thinks."

Tommy took a deep controlling breath and reminded himself it was just a game—a game for little kids at that—he didn't need to get so steamed about it.

"So what's my prize?"

"I'm gonna let you kiss me," Roy said with a big, devious smile.

"Yeah?" Tommy asked, thinking he was being put on. "All right, I guess I'll take the consolation prize then."

"That leaves me with the grand prize by default."

And he leaned in, and as sweet as anything Tommy had experienced in his whole life, Roy kissed his slightly parted lips. Even when Tommy stiffened, Roy did not pull back. Instead, slowly and deliberately, he gathered Tommy to him with a hold that was loose enough for him to escape from, but tight enough to be a real, romantic embrace. He kissed Tommy until he had to draw breath, and even then he did not let him go all the way.

"You... really wanted to?" Tommy asked, his head spinning. In that moment he had a single, solitary regret. It wasn't coming out here to shoot arrows, and it wasn't that he hadn't pulled out of Roy's embrace or even that he'd been kissed. It was that he hadn't kissed Roy first. Because Tommy liked the kissing. A lot. And he wanted to do it more.

Roy was just chastising him for being an idiot, telling him of course he wanted to, hadn't he been standing there when it happened, when Tommy grabbed him round the waist and kissed him full on the lips.

"Yes," Tommy told him.

"Yes?" Roy asked.

"Yes, I want my prize."

"Take it," Roy told him. "It's yours."

CHAPTER 7

"DON'T WORRY about it," Uncle Jacob told her in a kind, slow drawl. "Happens to the best of us."

Autumn sat in the back of Uncle Jacob's old Cadillac, counting streetlights as they moved slowly past. She didn't think they were going the speed limit, but she didn't say this.

She'd done as her mother requested and eaten, and within ten minutes, she'd thrown up on herself trying to get to a trashcan or bathroom. Mama called Jacob—who was Mama's uncle and who lived close by the hospital with Aunt Vivian—and, apologizing, asked if he could come get Autumn and let her stay with them for the night.

"I told her that I didn't want to eat," she murmured miserably. Her stomach was settled now, or rather, there was no danger that she was going to throw up again because there was nothing in there for her to lose. But she was being slowly carted away from Great-Pop and her waiting-room vigil, and she was sad and angry about it.

"What's that, sweets?" Uncle Jacob had a hearing aid, and it didn't work particularly well.

"I don't have anything to wear," Autumn called up to the front seat, not wanting to let him see how mad she was at Mama for making her leave.

"We'll get you a shower and a nightshirt and Aunt Vi can wash your pretty outfit for you. Don't worry."

Except of course she was worried! What if her Roy story wasn't enough? What if God or Jesus (whichever one was listening to prayers today) didn't think she cared enough about Great-Pop and they went ahead and called him home? She didn't want him to die. She wanted him to stay with her and with the family and keep on telling her stories and playing their games. If he would just get better, she would get on the swing and let him push her until she was thirty. She'd do it in front of Hannah and the whole school if that's what it took. She just wanted him to be okay.

When they arrived at the house, Autumn climbed out of the car. It was in a neighborhood so old it didn't even have a name. She didn't thank Uncle Jacob for coming to get her, even though she could hear Mama in the back of her head telling her that she should. Instead, she followed him through the screen door into the house where his five mutts started to bark and howl and jump up on her, dragging their nails down her legs in their excitement. It was a blur of brown and white and black and red and tan fur as the dogs swarmed her.

"Down! Down, you damned dogs!" Uncle Jacob bellowed, his hand flying to his ear. They were probably overloading his hearing aid.

But Autumn sank down onto the floor and let them lick her and lick the dried vomit off the front of her blouse. She tried to hug the wriggling mass of animals to her all at once. She wanted to sleep in a pile of dogs.

After herding the dogs downstairs, their barks only partially muted behind closed doors, Uncle Jacob brought her one of his old T-shirts, which went all the way down to her knees, and showed her to the guest bathroom as if she hadn't spent many an afternoon in this house as a child.

"Here's your towels and your washcloths and baby powder if you use it."

Autumn nodded. She only needed the towel, but she didn't tell him that.

"And there's soap on the rack. Just go ahead and put your clothes in the hamper and Vi will get to it in the morning."

"Okay." And then, because at her core she really was polite, even in the worst of times, she managed, "Thank you, Uncle Jacob." It wasn't his fault Mama had made her come. And it wasn't his fault she didn't want to be here. And, though she tried not to admit it, even in her head, she was really, really tired, and one of Aunt Vivian's pristinely made beds with its thick, fuzzy comforter and stiff, clean sheets sounded nice.

When Uncle Jacob was gone and she'd locked the door, Autumn slowly peeled off her clothes and drew a steaming hot bath. Then, as the tub was filling up, she got down a towel and a washcloth. She didn't like to use washcloths, preferring to soap up with her hands, but Aunt Vivian believed that if you didn't scrub with a cloth, you weren't really clean. If she could leave a damp washcloth over the side of the tub, she would at least give an impression of cleanliness that would satisfy Aunt Vivian's standards.

The water was almost too warm as she slipped into the large white tub, and she had to hold herself aloft and very gingerly sink down. Once submerged, however, Autumn felt her whole body relax just a little bit. She put her head under the water, wanting to get the hairspray out of her hair, and when she came up, the air felt cold on her face.

She thought about Great-Pop climbing that tree, and she wondered if things would have been different if Roy hadn't cheated at their game. But then Roy would have given him the prize honestly, and he'd have announced it just the same. *I'm going to let you kiss me.* Were they in love after they kissed? That was how it worked in the movies.

Autumn thought this was very romantic, and she laid her head against the side of the tub and tried to imagine what it was like to fall in love. When her best friend, Emma, told her that Hunter wanted to kiss her, she was really nervous. Emma said that Hunter said some of the guys in his class had dared him to do it, and if Autumn wouldn't, he was going to look like a coward.

It was a dumb reason to give away her first kiss, and she told Hunter so, even though she kissed him. He wasn't nearly as cute as Joey Sullivan, but he was cute enough, and he was always nice to her.

One time when she had to speak in front of the class, she got really sick and had to run out to the bathroom. She hadn't actually thrown up, just laid her head on her arms on the toilet seat and waited for her stomach to settle. When she got back, everyone called her Puke Girl, except Hunter. He asked if she was okay. So he was cute and he was nice and she thought, because of these things, that when they kissed under the basketball goal she was sure to fall in love.

But really there wasn't much to it. She closed her eyes; their lips touched. Or at least she thought they touched; the whole thing was really, really quick, and it didn't feel like much at all. She didn't fall right in love with Hunter, and when she went home that night, she wrote all about it in her journal, but she didn't put hearts around it or anything. And Joey Sullivan was still her favorite.

If he'd fallen in love because of the kiss or after it, Great-Pop was still really lucky to have that happen to him.

After she'd washed away all the sweat and ick of the long day and cleaned her hair so every last bit of hairspray was gone, Autumn unplugged the drain and sat in the tub until all of the dirty water was whisked away. Then she climbed out, careful to leave evidence of her washcloth (she'd only played with it, swirling it over the water until it became so heavy that it sank under the surface). She toweled off and dried her hair and brushed it out with an old brass-handled brush. She didn't like the bristles all that much, but if she didn't at least try to get the tangles out, she would wake up with her hair knotted in fifteen different places and standing out every which way.

Donning Uncle Jacob's old T-shirt, Autumn went to bed.

It was quiet in the guest room; the only sounds came from the clock down the hall, slowly ticking out the seconds. Aunt Vivian had drawn the curtains, but every time someone drove by, Autumn could see a streak of muted light that started at the corner of the window and went all the way across. She snuggled down into the fresh smelling pillow and said another small prayer.

"God, please let Great-Pop be okay."

She hoped that was good. She knew from her friends that there were all sorts of poems and speeches you were supposed to make when you addressed God—*Our father, who art in Heaven...*—except she and Mama didn't go to church, so she didn't know how to say them.

"God," she whispered into the still room, "I really love Great-Pop, and I don't want him to die."

Tears pricked her eyes, making them hot and painful. She was too tired to cry any more. "Please let him wake up tomorrow so that I can go talk to him. If you do, I'll...." She hesitated, trying to think what God might want from her.

She was still trying to think of something she could offer, a small piece of herself that might interest him, when she fell asleep.

CHAPTER 8

TOREN DECIDED to call his home Sunset Cottage and the forest surrounding it Sunset Forest because as long as he waited, and as much as he explored the boundaries of his property, the position of the sun in the sky never changed. He came to be certain that the gold light would never fade on his beautiful mass of stones and flowers. It comforted him in the deepest part of his heart. His home was bathed in sunset light, and it always would be. Assured of this, Toren began to feel the call of exploration.

He should pack dinner.

He looked over at the gold-dust gardener who moved like a phantom along the edge of his property, maybe growing things, maybe not. He didn't know if she could affect the world when he wasn't touching her. He thought about taking her hand, about asking her to assist in the kitchen. But she was the gardener, not the cook, and so when she looked up at him and smiled translucently, he only waved to her and walked to the house.

Toren had just set foot over the threshold when he heard the sound of plates clinking in the kitchen and the flow of slowly poured water.

His housekeeper!

A wide smile parted his lips. He hadn't been exceptionally lonely; if he had, he could have spent time with the gardener, such as her company would be. But he was strangely excited to see the woman who made his house smell of baking bread, even if she was a gold-dust phantom herself.

"Hello?" he called, not wanting to startle her. "Is that you, Miss…?" He again found himself hesitant to name her, even though he suddenly knew what he would call her: Reina.

He rounded the corner only to find that his housekeeper was not a bent old woman shuffling about his kitchen, but a young girl who stood on a stool to reach the sink. Her long red hair was braided down her back, and at odd intervals there stuck a blue or purple flower or a sprig of baby's breath. She turned to him and smiled prettily, her eyes green, her eyebrows pale.

"You're not my housekeeper?" he asked, though she was washing the dishes that he'd left out on the table. "You're wearing a circlet."

She raised a small, soapy hand to her forehead and giggled in surprise. "I guess I am!" she exclaimed and then went back to the dishes. She was different than the gold-dust gardener. She was real form and flesh. He even looked away from her and tried to ignore her before glancing back to see if she would fade. But real she remained.

"So you're a princess then?"

She shrugged at him, humming.

"I'm a princess who's also a housekeeper, I guess."

And he found this much more odd than the fact that the sunset light that shone on her young face and shoulders would never change. She bent her head low over her work.

"Who are you?"

"I…." She started strong and then her voice became quiet. "I'm not certain."

So he could name her! Or rather, he *had* named her. "Well then, you're Reina, my princess housekeeper."

"Oh!" she agreed, "I was worried I'd forgotten. You see, I opened my eyes, and here I was, and I couldn't remember a bit about how I got here. Only that maybe this isn't my real home but I'm glad to visit for a while, and I'm glad you remembered my name for me. I'm Reina!" And she asked, "And you are?"

"Toren, and this is my home."

"Yes, I figured that much at least."

"You really don't have to do my dishes, princess."

"It's all right," she argued, setting a sparkling clean platter onto the rack to dry. "When I woke up in my room, I thought, 'I really should do something about the mess.'"

"Your room?" He mused for a moment. "Where are you sleeping?"

"The closet upstairs," she said, as if it was nothing at all.

"The closet? But it's ragged, and there's hardly any furniture."

"I found myself there in a bed this morning. It's a little small, but it will do. Especially now that I've cleaned up in there."

"It certainly will *not* do," Toren argued. "A princess in my closet? No! I've got many, many rooms, and you can have your pick of any of them, even mine. Take it if you like, and I'll find somewhere else to sleep." He found he wanted her to be very happy and very comfortable.

She cast a pretty look at him over her shoulder. "I don't want to put you out in your own house, Toren."

"Well, it's not every day that I've got royalty doing my dishes. If you really mean to finish, then go pick your room when you're done. We'll fix it up for you anyway you like."

"All right," she agreed. "But Toren, do remember that I said I have another home. I won't be staying here all the time."

"What do you mean, princess?"

She thought about it for a second and set the glass alongside the dish. Then she dumped the rest of her dishwater down the drain, stepped off her stool, and plopped down upon it, sending plumes of shimmery silken material flying into the air. She was rather ungraceful for a princess, but pretty and polite and strangely regal despite the way she moved. He wanted to bow to her.

"Well, I think I'll come and go. Here, and then home."

"If you must," he agreed, slightly disheartened.

"I've got something to do there."

"What is that? And where is home for that matter? Through the forest?"

"I'm not sure," Reina replied with a faint smile, "but let's not worry about it too much. Right now I'm here! So, I'll go choose my room and, what will you do?"

"I was going to go exploring in the woods," he told her. "I want to see just how far the sunset extends, and I want to see how much of this land is mine. And really, I just want to see…." Everything.

"I'll make you some lunch to take along," she insisted and made him wait at the table while she busied herself in the cabinets and the cupboard. It was quite a sight, watching her march across the kitchen in her bare feet and ornate gown. She moved quickly as if she knew where everything was, and he wondered how long she'd been there and how often she left for her other home.

"There you go," she told him, putting the bag of goodies down in front of him. She appraised him for a second, and then a small worried crease formed between her eyebrows. "You need to be safe in the woods, Toren. I think it will be fine if you wander close, but I have a bad feeling about you going too far."

"You needn't worry about me! I'm capable of handling anything that comes my way." And he flashed her a charming smile.

Reina looked momentarily uncertain, and then with a little frown, she dipped one small hand into a hidden pocket in the folds of her skirt.

"This came for you. I found it underneath the door," she said, revealing an envelope with the seal broken. "I'm afraid I was very snoopy, and I've already read it, even though it wasn't addressed to me."

She sighed, hung her young head, and held it out.

"I have a *bad* feeling," she repeated, this time to her feet, and Toren took the letter and read it curiously, unfazed that she'd already taken a peek.

How are you enjoying the sunset? The cottage?

Join me, I've been waiting for you.

It's time.

And that was all it said.

"This doesn't even have my name on it anywhere," he argued. "We can't be certain it was meant for me."

"But isn't this your house?" she asked logically.

Toren just grinned, still confident about his never-ending sunset. Mystery letters did not trouble him in the least. "I'm off, Reina," he said boldly, "and if any more strange invites find their way under the door, simply throw them in the fire and pay them no mind at all. All right?"

"All right." She followed him into the living room and watched as he tossed the neatly folded letter into the fireplace.

CHAPTER 9

AUTUMN AWOKE in a room that was not her own, the covers kicked off the end of the bed, and her bare legs exposed. It took her a moment to realize where she was and another moment before she remembered Great-Pop. For that one happy, disoriented minute she didn't remember anything except parts of a strange dream. Autumn felt calm with herself and her surroundings and interested in starting her weekend. It made it that much more cruel when it all came back to her.

Sounds of clanking pots and pans and the rich smell of cooking batter enticed her out of bed and into the kitchen. Aunt Vivian was in her fluffy purple dressing gown and slippers with the embroidered roses on the toes. She moved very precisely as she made breakfast: spraying the cast-iron skillet, pouring batter onto the grill, poking at it with her spatula as it cooked. When she thought it was done enough, she flipped it, then pulled it off the heat, buttered the golden brown cake, and repeated the process.

Uncle Jacob sat at the end of the table with his coffee and the morning paper. He smiled at Autumn when she tiptoed into the kitchen.

"There's the sleepyhead."

"Good morning," Aunt Vivian said briskly, with a tight-lipped smile.

The pancakes smelled really good and Autumn's tummy rumbled in an inviting kind of way. She was hungry and thought she could keep her breakfast down.

"Good morning," Autumn replied and pulled out one of the dark-stained kitchen chairs. She waited only a moment, hoping someone would volunteer information before she asked. "What's going on with Great-Pop?"

Great-Pop was Aunt Vivian's father, and she always fussed about him. Uncle Jacob started to speak, but Aunt Vivian cut him off.

"He's out of the ICU, but he hasn't woken up."

"Is he in a coma?"

Aunt Vivian nodded stiffly. "We'll go see him later today."

"We can?" Autumn asked, barely controlling the excitement in her voice. All evening she'd been told *no, no, no,* but now…. Even if he wasn't awake, she felt certain if she could be near him and hold his hand and tell him that she loved him, he would hear her and understand and come back.

"This afternoon. I've got some things to do first."

Autumn bit her lip as she looked at the old clock that hung over the yellow flower wallpaper. It was only nine o'clock now. She knew Aunt Vivian and Great-Pop didn't always see eye-to-eye, but what was so important that she wouldn't want to go see her daddy in the hospital now?

"I've got a dress for you to wear," Vivian told her. "It was Jennifer's when she was your age. Your clothes are hanging on the line. But you can't go around in that old T-shirt all day."

"Thank you." Autumn managed to be polite. She didn't want to wear Aunt Jennifer's old dress, and she didn't want to wait. "Can I call my mom?"

"Your mother is at home, sleeping," Aunt Vivian told her sharply, and her end-of-discussion tone shut Autumn up. By the time Aunt Vivian laid them in front of her, Autumn had all but lost her appetite for pancakes, but Uncle Jacob's patient and gentle tone soothed her a bit.

"We'll go right at one o'clock," he promised her, "and meanwhile, you can play around the house."

"Outside," Vivian said, setting a glass of cold milk next to Autumn's untouched plate.

"Outside," Autumn agreed. She didn't want to be in the house anyway.

It turned out that Aunt Jennifer's old cotton sundress was really cool. It was vintage obviously with ties at the shoulders, but could have been something Autumn would have found in *Fashions* or *Style Girls.* Best of all, it was comfortable, which was really nice after spending the day with the elastic of her short-sleeved blouse cutting into her arms.

She walked around outside of the house with Uncle Jacob's dogs jumping and running and playing around her. They moved as a pack, though the leader always changed. Sometimes it was the smallest of the group that dictated where and how they played. They ran, as if playing tag, chasing each other, turning and then being chased. They rolled and knocked into one another and knocked into Autumn too, so more than once she fell to the ground in the bright summer grass.

Uncle Jacob and Aunt Vivian's property was not overly large, but it was open. Only the patio was fenced in, and there were pretty flowerbeds and good solid trees to climb. At the end of the property was the little playhouse Uncle Jacob had made himself. Aunt Jennifer's handprints were immortalized in the concrete step along with her name and her birth date. Autumn tried to go inside, but found it full of wasps, angry and looking to sting. She quickly shut the door and left the little house. It made her sad, though. Even though she was too old for the dolls and toy cookware, it would be cool to have her own space to hide in. It wasn't like anyone from school was around to see her here anyway.

After she'd circled the whole property, all the way down to the pink honeysuckle-covered chain link fence that marked the neighbors' plot, she found a place on the grass near one of the big trees and plopped down. The dogs ran past her, on to new adventures.

She tried to remember a Great-Pop and Roy story, a good one so she could tell it to herself. The only one that came to mind, though, was the saddest one. It was her least favorite, the one she wished Great-Pop had never told. She didn't want to think about it now. She put her chin on her knees and closed her eyes and felt the cool breeze move her hair.

"I'm sorry you had to die, Roy," she whispered. "If you were here, I know Great-Pop wouldn't leave you." And then with some surprise and dismay, she slowly opened her eyes.

Did Great-Pop want to go to Roy?

Her throat tightened and her hands began to shake. Did Great-Pop *want* to leave the family? To leave her? He was out of the ICU, and they could go in and visit him, but he wasn't awake. He wasn't fine. He wasn't at home.

She tried to think about the time Great-Pop and Roy went fishing down at the creek and Roy caught a great big catfish, or the night they got lost driving around in Roy's new Ford, or the time they got caught out in the rain and Roy promised that Great-Pop was always gonna be his guy. But they all flickered and faded in the face of the worst story. Wherever Roy was, surely he wanted Great-Pop with him too. But didn't he understand what Great-Pop meant to her? She wasn't ready to let go of him. There were so many more stories she needed to hear.

"I don't want him to leave," she whispered, and ran her hands through the grass, pulling up blades and tearing them to shreds.

Closing her eyes, she chastised herself, "Stop it, Autumn. He's not trying to take Great-Pop from you."

More grass, great handfuls now, and the story started to come despite her frantic efforts to make it stop.

They were in their twenties now.

They were having a picnic in an orchard.

Roy was laying his head in Tommy's lap.

Tommy was laughing and talking about the future.

Roy was being really quiet, really serious.

He told Tommy he wished there was a place for them to be together.

Tommy said, "We are together."

And Roy said, "A cave. No, a valley, where no one would ever bother us, and we could do whatever we pleased."

Tommy really liked this, and he told Roy so.

And they drank more wine and Roy fell asleep and when Tommy tried to wake him—

"NO!" AUTUMN shouted, standing up and flinging the grass so hard and aimlessly that she hurt her elbow. "No, no, *no!*" She kicked the ground. She hated that story. She hated it, and she didn't want to think about it. Not now, not with Great-Pop in the hospital. Roy could wait. He'd waited fifty years; he could wait longer. He could wait forever!

She took off running toward the house, her sandals flopping loudly as she rounded the side. The dogs caught her movement and came running over in an excited pack to see what all the fuss was about.

She ran through the carport and up the steps and flung open the screen door, even though Aunt Vivian had specifically instructed her to stay outside.

When she got to the kitchen, the air-conditioning hit her in the face, and she gulped it in by the stale, cold lungful.

"Autumn?" Aunt Vivian called. She sounded displeased, but Autumn didn't care. She would go to the guest room and sit quietly or try to go back to sleep, but she didn't want to be out in the yard, under the trees.

"I'm sorry, Aunt Vivian," she said, as calmly as she could. She could feel the heat in her face. "I don't want to play anymore."

Aunt Vivian had gotten dressed for the day in a pair of pink slacks and a white cotton shirt. She looked as tight and put-out as ever, except her eyes were now red-rimmed. It startled Autumn, who had never in her life seen Aunt Vivian cry. She took a hesitant step forward and said, "I'm sorry."

Her aunt waved her off and swiped a knuckle under her eye.

"He's going to be okay," Autumn said as authoritatively as she could. And yet she was very aware that she was twelve and Aunt Vivian was sixty. There was no weight to her words.

For a long moment Aunt Vivian studied her, fingering the gold cross around her neck, and then, very slowly, as if it pained her to speak, she asked, "Do you want to look at some photographs with me?"

CHAPTER 10

THE SUNLIGHT extended deep into the woods, and Toren found his path pleasantly illuminated. The venerable trees stretched upward, canopies offered to the heavens. They were great climbing trees, with low-hanging branches and great ugly knobs for footholds.

As he journeyed away from Sunset Cottage, following the long creek, Toren found himself stopping at times to climb a tree that was too tempting to pass up. And then because he felt compelled to do so, he would scoot out along a high branch and leap from one tree to the next, catching the other's branch at the last possible second and pulling himself up. There was a thrill to it—to tree climbing. When he grew tired of one tree, he leaped down to the forest floor and resumed journeying, following the bank of the creek, until he found the next one.

He walked like that for hours, trailing his fingertips over the rough bark of the trees, whistling to birds as they sang their songs, and stopping in the clearing to eat one of the many delicious offerings Princess Reina had packed for him. Every time he passed a berry bush, he'd collect the fruit and put it in his pack to bring back to the cottage. Maybe Reina could make him a pie.

The forest was every bit as magnificent as he'd hoped, and he decided, as he did with all things now, that the trees were his. Anything that the sunset light fell on was his. He'd seen no other dwellings or property signs or even the hint of another person to dissuade him.

The forest did not turn dark until he reached the place from which the creek sprang. There was a small rock face, about double his height, with a slow-flowing waterfall that fed down into the creek bed. As if the wall marked the boundary of the sunset, purple-gray shadows bruised the ground, and what he could see past that spot was a night sky, stark against the remnants of the sunset.

"Someone else's territory," he decided to himself, though curiosity begged him to at least climb the slippery rock face and look over the edge. "I wonder," he murmured.

What lay beyond?

Was it always night there?

Was there more sunset territory past this spot?

Toren gripped the first jutting rock and checked his footing. It was slick with years and years of collected slime, and he had to move very carefully, choosing only the least damp holds to grab. It wouldn't be much of a fall, but it would be embarrassing to return home covered in creek mud, nonetheless.

Slowly he climbed until his copper-curled head crested the edge of the wall. There he could see a vast clearing and a giant, glimmering lake. Turning his face up, he realized it wasn't night there at all. The sun hung suspended in the sky, but it was masked by thick clouds that poured rain. The effect of the gray sky with shafts of white sunlight streaming through was almost as beautiful as the golden rays of light and the fiery-red sun on his side of the forest.

This rain was the source of his creek. As the lake overflowed, it spilled out into a small river, which fed right into his waterway.

He continued to gaze over the edge of the rock face and wondered if he mightn't go just a little farther. Just then a bird flew down from one of the tall pine trees which edged the clearing and, Toren swore, dove right for him.

"Get away from me, you damned crow!" he cried, waving the bird off. But his motion caused Toren to lose his grip on the rock, and he tumbled off the face of it straight into the water. His clothes were instantly soaked through with creek muck, just as he'd feared. The crow swooped up into the air, its two-foot wingspan blocking his vision for a moment. Then it dove again, right at him. The bird landed heavily on his chest, its black feet splayed, and cocked its head to one side to stare at him with a jet-black, glassy eye. He could see his reflection in the eye. When it turned its great bird head to the other side, Toren saw that its other eye was not black but the deep, endless red of love or rage; he couldn't tell which.

And then it leaped off of him and began to hop along the creek bed, pecking at the ground.

Toren stood slowly, wringing out what he could from his clothing.

"What the hell was that about?" he demanded of the beastly bird. "You didn't want me in the Rain Kingdom?"

The bird ignored him.

"Well, you don't have to worry, crow, because I don't have any plans to intrude on your rainy day."

Slinging his pack over his damp shoulder, Toren started toward home, annoyed that he would have to trudge for hours in this mess. There was no way to alert Reina either, even if she had not yet gone to her other home. There would be no hot bath waiting for him. Stupid crow.

He stomped on and on, ignoring the trees that had once thrilled him, muttering to himself instead and kicking at the rocks that lined the path.

He was almost back to the last thicket when he heard a loud squawk behind him. Toren realized with annoyance that the crow, which he'd been cursing under the name Red-Eye, was following him.

"What do you want?" he demanded. "First you knock me off the wall, then you stand on me, now you're following me! If it's food you're after, you can't have any of mine!"

The crow pecked at the ground, and then looked up at him from a low bow, its blood eye turned on him.

"And you can't have my soul either," he warned, certain the beast bird had nefarious intentions.

Red-Eye hopped in a little circle, turning away from him and chasing an anole along the bank.

"All right then," he said firmly and started back on his journey, but it wasn't long before he saw the crow soar past him and land in the same trees he'd climbed only hours before. It would wait, watching him walk, and then it would spread its great wings and swoop into the next distant tree. And in this manner, the bird followed him all the way to the well.

"I've got a mind to go in my cottage and find something to kill you with," Toren warned the bird heavily. He couldn't recall any real weapons in the cottage, save for the knives in the kitchen. He wondered if Reina would be too offended if he used her cookware for avian slaughter.

Red-Eye perched on the low wooden fence and folded his wings into his body, turning and presenting a very handsome profile. For one so rude, he was a fine-looking bird.

"You'd better not be here when I return."

Reina was not in the house when he entered, and he was grateful for this as he tracked mud and dried dirt clods across her clean floor. He could only imagine her in her royal finery, down on the floor with a scrub bucket, cleaning up his foolishness. Upstairs, he found a note on the door of the room next to his. In pretty cursive scrawl it said, *This one please.* He pushed the door open to reveal what had been the purple room. It was now pink—everywhere, princess pink. There was a large canopy bed and a striking, double-doored wardrobe with intricate pearl inlay. Where had these things come from? At the window seat, there was a new flowerbox full of vibrant pink flowers and delicate little spider-webbed vines. It was a room fit for a princess, and so he kept his muddy feet at the door and did not muss her rug.

As he'd imagined, there was not a hot bath waiting for him in the tub upstairs. So he found his gold-dust gardener and had her help him drag water up from the well many, many times, to heat it on the stove. It was ages before the tub was full. Each time he walked outside, he found Red-Eye just a hop closer to the well. Even when he swung his empty bucket at the bird, it did not flinch but instead watched him.

As the gardener poured the last bucket of hot water into the bath, Toren released her back into dust.

He had just stepped into the blissfully hot bathwater when Red-Eye flew to the bathroom window and landed on the outer sill.

"Are you serious?" Toren bellowed at the creature and, grappling for his dirty shoe, he threw it at the glass. But it did not break. Instead the shoe bounced perfectly off the unlocked pane, which then swung inward just enough to allow the crow entry.

"What do you want?"

He was determined now that should the bird come within grabbing distance, he would drown it or break its neck.

"My master approaches," it said, opening its black beak just enough to let sound past.

For a perplexed moment Toren only stared. When he found his voice he asked, not *How do you speak?* but, "Who is your master?"

"My master comes to claim you."

This immediately sent a hot flash of anger through Toren. He thought of the invitation he had thrown into the fire, the one he'd assured Reina was not for him. "Your master comes to claim me?" he repeated. "By what right?"

The bird only stared at him.

"You tell your master that if he sets foot in my Sunset Forest, I will be forced to defend it."

"My master comes to claim you, To-To-To-" Each syllable sounded like "Taw" and he realized the bird was attempting to say his name.

"Toren," he replied. "Tell your master that Toren grants no audience, and he is not welcome here. I will not venture into the Rain Kingdom as long as he stays out of my sunset."

"My master approaches, Toren," the bird repeated, undeterred, and Toren grabbed the other shoe and hurled it at the hulking avian. It squawked and rose into the air, flying out through the open window, leaving only sleek black feathers in its wake. One floated in his bath water for a moment before sinking under the surface.

CHAPTER 11

WHEN AUTUMN returned to the hospital with Aunt Vivian and Uncle Jacob, the waiting room on Great-Pop's floor was crowded with the familiar faces of her relatives. Mama was right that she shouldn't worry about Great-Pop having family support—it seemed everyone they'd ever known had turned out to visit. There were aunts and uncles and cousins and second cousins and people who might be third cousins or might not be related at all. Friends of the family had shown up, some bringing their children along. Tiny babies, some sleeping, some screaming, were passed from hand to hand so it was impossible to tell which child belonged where. There was a group of little kids gathered in the corner, the smallest playing with the waiting room toys, some of the older ones engrossed in their handheld video games. Hannah, thankfully, was nowhere to be seen.

Autumn moved through the group, catching snippets of conversation as she went.

"Work's a bitch, but what are you going to do? I can't quit, not if I want to keep my health insurance," one aunt said to her friend, or maybe it was a cousin? She was bouncing a toddler on her hip.

"Every day I think about telling them all to stuff it, but— Andrew!" she snapped, whipping her head around to chastise a redheaded boy with freckles. He was poking his older sister with a wicked grin on his little imp face. "If you don't stop terrorizing your sister, I'm going to come over there and bust your butt!" And then as if she hadn't ever stopped talking about work, she turned back and said, "But you know? Some days the boss can be almost kind of sweet. Doesn't hurt that he's sexy."

Autumn's grandmother motioned her close and scooped her into a one-armed hug. Autumn hugged her back and listened to her tell the neighbor from down the street a story she'd heard a hundred times before.

"Dad used to pile us all in the back of his truck and take us to the library every Saturday morning. I was in charge of making sure we didn't lose any books on the highway. Vivian was the lookout for the police. She'd call out if she saw them, and we'd all throw ourselves flat in the back and wait until we got the all clear. I honestly don't think they would have cared, not like they do now, but she was really serious about her job. Anyway, this one time we're going to the library and Dad sees this man stranded on the side of the road, with steam coming out of the hood of his car—"

Autumn listened to the story as if she were hearing it for the first time. This was what they all needed to be talking about—how cool Great-Pop was, how much he did for people. She looked around the room at her relatives. After she got her time to visit with him, maybe she would go around and ask others to share their stories too.

"—had us all helping!" Her grandmother laughed. "When we got to the library, we looked like little grease monkeys, covered in dirt and grime, and I don't know what else. And of course the librarians are looking at us like we're dirt poor, but Dad just walks up with all our books and asks as charming as can be, 'You have any books on getting grease out of fabric? I'd hate for their mom to come home and see 'em all like this.'"

Aunt Vivian appeared nearby, sour-faced as ever, and Autumn walked over to her. She was hoping that despite their late arrival, they would still be able to go in. There was almost too much family present. Autumn was frightened she wouldn't get her chance to see Great-Pop. Aunt Vivian assured her they would get their turn.

Before going to the hospital, they'd spent some time looking through the old, yellowed photo albums which Aunt Vivian kept in a place of honor on her bookshelf. Each page creaked as it turned over the rusted rings of the binder, and many of the plastic covers flapped open, photos sliding around. Aunt Vivian did not keep her pictures in one of those pocketed photo albums with its clean, tight plastic and lines for writing notes. Instead, she had to peel back the plastic at odd intervals to flip the photo and read the inscription. She did this many, many times and when she replaced the photo, she did so precisely, careful to press down the plastic so no bubbles showed—even though the page had lost most of its stick.

Autumn learned that many of the people in the pictures were dead, as Aunt Vivian liked to point out this trait the most. But she was a good storyteller too, and if she remembered something interesting about a person (beyond their being deceased) she would offer it readily.

"She got married to an Italian boy who only wanted her for the green card."

"He was a gambler and a drunk."

"Her son killed himself."

"She was a crazy that used to drag her neck along the clothesline." (When Autumn asked what this meant, Aunt Vivian raised an eyebrow and repeated, *she used to drag her neck along the clothesline.*)

"He had her cremated, even though her mother wanted her buried proper."

"She heard voices from the time she was five."

"Sad. He was crawling under the fence with his shotgun, and it went off."

"I don't have any idea who that is."

"Or him."

"Or her."

"Wait, no, I do know her. She's the one with the little half-black grandbaby."

"We're not sure what happened to her. One day she went to the store, and she never came back."

"He used to sell ice cream down at the park back before it became such a bad place."

Actually, all of Aunt Vivian's stories were kind of depressing.

She would describe landscapes as they used to be, though, and Autumn liked that a lot. She'd talk about stores and parking lots as open fields and groves. With her stories, Aunt Vivian built schoolhouses and libraries in the place of chain supermarkets, and thinking about them took Autumn's mind off Great-Pop for a while.

Until they turned to that old black-and-white photo of the two young men.

"This is Daddy," Aunt Vivian said offhandedly, no fancy story to go along with the photo. She was about to turn the page when Autumn stuck out her hand to block it.

"Wait," she said. "Who is that with him?"

Aunt Vivian studied the photograph for a moment. On the left, Great-Pop was smiling, a smear of freckles popping even in the black-and-white photograph. He had curly hair and a strong, handsome face. Next to him was another young man, dark-haired, with a devilish smile. He had his arm slung over Great-Pop's shoulders, like they were good friends. Autumn didn't dare breathe as she waited for Aunt Vivian to peel back the plastic.

She knew the inscription would say it was Tommy and Roy; it had to. She stared at the picture, burning the image into her memory, until Aunt Vivian finally pulled it off the sticky paper and turned it over. Autumn's eyes moved to her mama's aunt and she waited, breathless.

"Doesn't say."

"Can I have it?" Autumn burst out at almost the same time. She suddenly, desperately, *needed* the photograph.

For a long moment Aunt Vivian studied her, as if she understood just how important the photo was to Autumn. And then, wordlessly, she placed it onto the photo page and sealed it back up in plastic. She continued to show off her photographs, weaving another ten or fifteen tales of misery, but Autumn had lost all interest. She nodded occasionally, no longer knowing or caring what she was nodding at.

"Are you ready, Autumn?" Aunt Vivian asked, startling Autumn, who had been twirling her thumbs around faster and faster trying to go as quick as possible without bumping them together. She blinked and saw that her aunt and uncle were standing, ready to go into Great-Pop's room. She immediately hopped off the chair and followed along behind them, wishing Mama didn't have to work that Saturday.

She'd wanted this for so many hours, and now that it was happening, she was a little scared.

She wished Aunt Vivian had let her have the picture. She wanted to show it to Great-Pop and ask him if that was Roy in the photograph.

She'd expected Great-Pop's room to be something large and attractive. The last romantic movie she saw with Emma, the heroine had fallen into a coma, and her hospital room was the size of Autumn's bedroom. The windows opened, and the breeze caught the sheer green curtains and played with them. And there were lots and lots of flowers. Of course, then the hero of the story came in and sat next to her bed and talked with her and held her hand and told her that he loved her and he was sorry she'd fallen off his motorcycle. That's all it took. He said he was sorry, and she opened her eyes, and they kissed. It was really romantic.

But there was little romance in Great-Pop's hospital room. For one thing, he had a roommate, separated from him only by an opaque curtain. And any time one of them accidentally rustled it, the other man let out a swearword and called for the nurse to come and take them away. The room was also small with only one chair for sitting, and it was occupied by another of Great-Pop's children staying long past his allotted time.

Autumn had a difficult time getting close to the bed, and when she finally pushed past Uncle Jacob, who patted her on the head, she wished she had not been in such a rush. Great-Pop was not lying peacefully in the bed as if sleeping. The window was not open, and no breeze played with the curtains. He looked wrinkled and pale and lifeless, and there were tubes and wires sticking out of him. The monitor next to his bed beeped insistently, and there were a couple of bags hanging on a metal stand. One dripped fluid into an IV in his hand; the other, she didn't know. She couldn't even find a good way to hold his hand because she was worried about the IV in his vein. And there were so many people around. How was she supposed to tell him a story with so many people around her?

She looked up at Aunt Vivian, who was fighting tears and glaring at the same time.

Autumn moved just a little closer to Great-Pop.

"We're here, Dad," Uncle Jacob said a little too loudly. The man in the bed next to Great-Pop's began to grumble.

"Jacob, turn your hearing aid up," Uncle Greg said from the chair he should have vacated for another sibling.

"What?" Jacob asked, turning to his wife's brother.

"Daddy," Aunt Vivian whispered, her pink-painted lips pursing so tightly they almost disappeared in on themselves.

"Hi, Great-Pop," Autumn whispered, reaching out and touching his shoulder. She didn't like it, didn't like how still he was. She wanted him to stir underneath her touch.

"I said, turn your hearing aid up," Uncle Greg called, and Uncle Jacob laughed, again a little too loud.

"Nurse!" the neighbor bellowed and began to press his buzzer insistently.

"I can't believe—" Aunt Vivian's voice caught in her throat, and she let out a shuddering breath.

"That better?" Uncle Jacob asked, his voice still a bit loud.

"Almost," Uncle Greg agreed.

"Nurse!"

"I can't believe you would *do this to me*," Aunt Vivian snapped, deciding then to give into the fear and anger welling within her.

"Once upon a time," Autumn whispered frantically, "you and Roy got married in the vineyard. It wasn't a real wedding because there wasn't a pastor. But there was a ring and—"

"Autumn, honey, can you move so that Vi can get closer to Great-Pop?" Uncle Jacob asked kindly. She looked at Uncle Jacob, not understanding. No, she had to tell the story. She had to tell the story, or he wasn't going to get any better!

"You still owe me an apology, Daddy," Aunt Vivian ground out between her teeth, her lips curled and snarling like a dog. "Don't you dare die on me without giving me my apology!"

"And that's when he said he loved you for the first time," Autumn whispered as quickly as she could.

"Nurse!" the man bellowed. "Get these goddamned people out of my room!"

"Autumn, come back here?" Uncle Jacob tried again, and in that moment a stern looking nurse appeared in the doorway. She was the size of two grown women, and she had her fists dug into her ample hips. She had turned toward the roommate to chastise him for wasting her time when she saw, with those eagle eyes of hers, that there were *four* people crammed into the small space on the other side of the room.

"Just what do you think this is?" she asked loudly, addressing the four of them with a withering look. "You people have been told that it's two visitors at a time. So either two of you skedaddle, or all four of you will be back in the waiting room."

Uncle Jacob grabbed Autumn's arm in a strong grip and began to pull her from the room.

"No!" she cried in protest. "No! No! I'm not done telling my story! Please!"

But Uncle Jacob continued to pull on her, and when she dug her heels in, he grabbed her under both armpits as if she were a toddler and hoisted her up off the ground.

"Uncle Greg already had his turn!" she cried. "And Aunt Vivian is just yelling at him! Let me go! I need to tell my story!"

He ignored her until they were out in the hallway, and then he set her down firmly.

"Now, Autumn," he started, but she didn't give him a chance to finish. She tore down the hall, running... where? It didn't matter. Anywhere! She couldn't go back to the room to tell her story, and she didn't want to go back to the waiting room. It wasn't fair. It wasn't fair! Uncle Greg had his turn; he was being selfish! And Aunt Vivian didn't even deserve to have Great-Pop as her father, and she didn't deserve to have the photograph either! And in that moment she hated them all.

She flung open the door to the stairwell and began to run down flight after flight of stairs until she hit the exit and burst out into the smoking courtyard. Nurses in their colorful and friendly looking scrubs stood around pulling drags off their cigarettes while they gossiped. There were a couple of doctors too, white coats and stethoscopes and cigarettes in their hands. They ignored Autumn as she ran across the gravel path up toward the other building.

They didn't even let me tell my story!

She searched frantically for a place to sit. Not at one of the old benches covered in bird crap, but somewhere private and hidden. Somewhere like that brick corner where the two walls met. There were bushes there, and just enough space for a young girl to fit and hide from the whole world. She was going to tell her story. Autumn just hoped she was close enough to Great-Pop that he could feel her words, even if he could not hear them.

CHAPTER 12

"THIS IS silly," Tommy said. They'd driven all the way down to Herdford County to the vineyards, because Roy said he wanted to eat grapes off the vine. They'd parked along the dirt road down by the willow trees, and then snuck over the wire fence into the back part of the vineyards. Now, they walked along the rows of grape plants, all curling up over their posts. Roy pulled out bunches and examined them. He was picky about which grapes to get off the vine, and he took a good long time choosing one. When finally he plucked one, he popped it into Tommy's mouth and kissed him before he could chew the grape.

"I want to marry you," he said, and when Tommy made to protest, he put another grape into his mouth. "I don't want to hear what you have to say, Tom Johnson. I understand that a union of our souls isn't something the state or the Lord is gonna condone. But I still want to."

Tommy didn't say anything, but Roy put another grape in his mouth anyway, letting his fingers linger for a second on his lips.

"I love you."

Tommy smiled as vibrant as the sun and then chewed his grapes. He'd been thinking it for a while too, that he loved Roy, he just hadn't been brave enough to say it. He wished he'd said it first.

"And I just think if we're going to keep on doing what we're doing—" Tommy flushed at these words like an embarrassed schoolboy. "—then I want to make it an honest commitment. Y'know? We don't need a church wedding. You and I'd both look silly in white veils anyway. But I still want to marry you."

"Where should we go?" Tommy asked.

"Don't have to go anywhere."

"You sure? Maybe there's somewhere out West?"

"Don't have to go *anywhere*," Roy repeated, taking Tommy's reluctant hand and uncurling his fingers with fine and gentle strokes.

When his palm finally lay flat, Roy reached into his pocket and laid a ring right in the middle of Tommy's hand.

"This is—"

"It was my daddy's," Roy said, "and when he died, my momma got so mad at him for leaving us that she threw it in the pond behind our house and cursed his name. Well, then she cried for a week because she wanted it back. So I did what any good son would do. I waded through that muck from sunup to sundown, and I found it for her."

"But here it is."

"Here it is. Because she wasn't crying over the ring, she was crying over him being gone. I was just too young and dumb to realize it. So I took it and kept it in case she got mad again. If I had it, she couldn't throw it."

Herdford County was in the middle of hill country, and the vineyard was surrounded by the gentle brushstroke of green rolling hills. The animals that grazed along the slopes were like small white and black and brown blobs of paint. They were right in the middle of a painting.

"You sure about this, Roy? You won't ever be able to tell anyone I'm your husband," Tommy said.

Roy shrugged, unconcerned.

"Won't be able to take me to parties and introduce me around. Won't even be able to buy a house with me, unless we go to the city and get an apartment together and pretend to be brothers."

"Why are you worrying about something like that?"

"Because." Gently he turned the polished silver in his hand. "Doesn't that mean anything to you?"

"Not being able to do those things? Nah, it doesn't mean a thing to me. What are you saying, Tommy? Does it mean something to you?"

"Well, don't you want to, I don't know, find a wife or something, so you have someone to keep on your arm?"

"You're an idiot." And it was the first time he'd ever seen Roy look really, truly sour with him. "You're a complete flippin' idiot if you think I'd rather marry some girl in town so that I can go to dinner parties than be with you. I don't care what they know or don't know. I don't need 'em to know about us to make what we have real. But if you do...." He took a deep and controlling breath, and he hesitated for a moment. "Give me the ring back."

With a heavy heart, Tommy handed the silver ring over, but instead of pocketing it or throwing it or turning with it and leaving Tommy to himself, Roy slipped it on his own finger. He held it up and wiggled his fingers like those ditzy girls when they got engaged. It made Tommy laugh.

"I'll wear this. I'll give you something else."

And he produced from his other pocket a chess piece. Tommy took it and held it up to the light, turning it once and then twice before recognition kicked in. "You stole it from the library!"

"I did."

"Huh." Tommy laughed, and then the sound of it stilled on his lips as he flipped the piece over and saw on the bottom where Roy had carefully carved the words *I love you.*

"I will take you out west to this fabled town where we can be out in the open together, if that's what you need. If you won't even consider marrying me before then."

"You're an idiot too," Tommy told him, and grabbed the front of his shirt and pulled him into a sweet kiss. It tasted like grapes. "I wasn't saying *that.* I wasn't saying I wouldn't marry you. I was thinking *for* you, Roy. And of course I wish there was somewhere we could go and they wouldn't ever trouble us, but I'm just worried that you—"

"Stop it."

"I just want your happiness."

"Stop it, Tommy. Tell me you're married to me."

For a long moment they stared at each other—Tommy's dark eyes on Roy's light ones. And then Tommy laid his head against Roy's chest and slowly breathed out. He was still tightly gripping the fabric of Roy's shirt in both hands. "I'm married to you," he promised, and meant it with everything in his heart.

Roy nudged the side of his face with his nose. "I'm married to you too."

CHAPTER 13

IT WAS strange to be over at Great-Pop's house when Great-Pop still wasn't home. It was almost as if he was just in the other room, or he'd stepped out to get something from the grocery store. Autumn kept looking up during their visit with Great-Mom, expecting to see him there. She and Mama and Grandma brought over dinner after Mama got off work, and at first Autumn was expected to stay close by, visiting. But after no one had addressed her for almost twenty minutes, she decided to go exploring around the house and Mama didn't protest.

There used to be a little room with a toy box in it down the hall from the spare bedroom. Great-Mom had a big writing desk there where she paid her bills, and there was an ugly old chair and a large bookshelf too. As long as Autumn could remember, a white-painted crib sat right under the cuckoo clock on the opposite wall. Sometimes there were as many as three babies snuggled down in the crib at the same time. With a family as large as theirs, someone was always having another baby.

Running her hands along the well-used crib, Autumn let out a long, low sigh. She couldn't remember sleeping there, of course, but she could definitely remember playing in this room.

What are you doing, princess?

She could hear him as if he were actually there. She was five years old, and Great-Pop's voice was pleasant but also edged with the sort of suspicion that was standard when playing babysitter to a young child. Autumn looked up at him, her eyes widening with surprise. She'd been exploring the house in her frilly skirt and the tights with little red hearts on them. The seam stuck off the toes, and she used to pull and pull on it until there was a long piece of string that Mama had to cut off.

"Princess?" he asked again.

Great-Pop was an imposing figure in the doorway, shadowed and looming. And Autumn, who was very scared of her great-grandparents because they were so old, fell back just a little.

"I'm not doing anything! At all!" she lied. She'd been messing with the bookshelf. *World Books* from the sixties with their cream and green covers lay open all around her. She looked down at her crime. At his disbelieving silence, she relented.

"Readin' stories," she mumbled. "Just readin' all the stories."

Really she was just looking at the pictures, and she hadn't found very many pretty ones yet. There were lots with soldiers and some people with signs looking angry. She did like a big black-and-white photograph of a woman with long hair, flowers at her temples. She wore silly clothes, but she was pretty, and her mouth was open like she was singing. Autumn flipped the page.

"Oh yeah?" Great-Pop asked. "Do you have scissors?"

Autumn remembered when Hannah had to go into timeout for using a pair of scissors on a library book. No scissors allowed near the books! She quickly shook her head.

Sometimes she would read aloud the words she knew or could sound out. There were a whole lot of "cats" in the encyclopedia—even if some of the cats were in the middle of larger words, like *abdicate*. A-B-D-I-*cat*-E.

"So, what are the stories about?" Great-Pop asked, gesturing to the open book.

"Princesses," she said, flipping the page. There were too many words printed there, so she flipped the page again. Autumn didn't need a crown to make up a story about a princess—all it took was a pretty woman with an elegant smile. Her young brain was always on royalty. She loved stories about fancy tiaras and ponies and handsome princes. When she grew up, she was going to be a princess. Then when she was old—like thirteen or fourteen—she would marry her prince, and then she would live in a castle and she would have fifty maids, and they would all make her grilled cheese sandwiches any time she wanted.

Great-Pop sat in the old chair with its bright orange pleather seat and its wooden armrests. Great-Mom's typewriter sat on a little wobbly stand, and over the chair was a shelf Great-Pop made himself; Autumn had watched him hang it the year before. It held all of Great-Mom's little knick-knacks. Mama had stories about a bunch of them. Autumn's favorite was the thick glass egg. Inside was a real flower that never died and never faded. They told her it was because no oxygen could get inside to make it wilt, but Autumn believed with all her heart that it was magic. Magic or no, though, she still wasn't allowed to touch it or any of the other amazing things on the shelf.

"'Cause they'll break?" she'd asked her mama as she eyed the collection.

"Because they'll definitely break," Mama had agreed.

As Autumn continued to look at the *World Book* in front of her, Great-Pop rocked in the chair, making it creak under his weight. Autumn glanced at him out of the corner of her eye and scowled. She didn't like that he was there. She was having fun by herself. She turned another page.

"I can tell you a story about a princess, if you like."

She blinked, and then looked up at him, a mixture of surprise and delight on her face. But there was room for disbelief. Daddy said he'd tell her a story every night if she would go to bed without complaining, but when she did, he just flipped off the light and left her there in the dark. So maybe Great-Pop just wanted her to put the *World Books* up. But he patted his knee and promised, "It's a story about Princess Autumn."

This was too much for her young heart to take. A story about a princess with her name? She leaped to her feet.

"Is she me?" she asked hopefully, and Great-Pop smiled at her.

"I guess you'll just have to find out, huh?"

Autumn jumped into his lap, and he let out a long "Oomph!" when she landed. "Does she have really, really long hair?"

"Are you going to let me tell this story or not?" he asked, and she nodded in fevered little jerks. "Okay. There once was a princess named Autumn, and she had the longest red hair you ever saw in your whole life. She kept it in a braid and put in flowers with little white bits of baby's breath and whatever else she felt like."

"Sapphires?" Autumn asked, because she loved sapphires.

"Absolutely," Great-Pop agreed. "And all the sapphires that she put in her hair came from the ocean."

She didn't blink.

"She had to dive down to the bottom of the ocean to find them all."

"Great-Pop?"

"Yes, Autumn?"

"I don't know how to swim," she whispered.

"Well, Princess Autumn does know how to swim," he promised.

"Because she listened to Miss Karen at swim practice? Can she put her head under the water?"

"That's right," he agreed. "She was very good at putting her head under the water. She could even hold her breath all the way to the bottom of the ocean."

"Where all the sapphires are."

After that story, Autumn fell head over heels in love with her Great-Pop, and she asked to visit him almost every day. Whenever her mother obliged, Autumn would run straight up to him and demand another story. He never failed to delight her. Sometimes he would tell her about Princess Autumn in her castle or her adventures in other lands. She always wanted to know about the dresses, and she wasn't content with just the color—she needed details and she would ask him questions upon questions until she was satisfied that Princess Autumn was perfectly attired. Poor Great-Pop. It never would do to have Princess Autumn dressed in the same gown twice, either—and Autumn had a memory that surprised her great-grandfather. She never forgot a dress, even when he did.

Sometimes he could get away with telling a story that wasn't about Princess Autumn. She would moan at first, but by the end she was entranced with his storytelling, losing herself in his words. When Great-Pop and Great-Mom were in a fight with their neighbor over a tree that had fallen on her property, Great-Pop told the story about scary Old Witch Crandal. When they got robbed the following summer, he told a funny story about a master jewel thief who eventually robbed himself!

As she grew older, Autumn went through a phase where all she wanted to hear were stories about adults when they were her age. It didn't matter if they were family or not—if she knew the adult well enough to ask, she would. *When you were a little kid...?* She wanted to know what they liked to do, where they went, what they ate, and especially about them getting in trouble. Maybe it was because she was a good girl who rarely found herself punished, but she just loved to hear stories about mischief. She asked Daddy, but he was always moody and would just snap at her or yell. Great-Pop told his stories without hesitation, and they were always wonderful. Like the time he'd sliced open the lettuce and when his stepmother found it all brown, he blamed it on his brother. And one time his sister got so mad she threw a beehive at their goat. Then she had both bees and a goat chasing her.

Great-Pop told her about the time he and his brother got the "whoopin' of a lifetime" after they tried to see if cow farts were flammable. Autumn's eyes grew wide as she imagined it.

"Ended up setting our good milk cow's tail on fire."

"Was the cow okay?" she asked and didn't laugh until after he assured her that the cow was fine, but neither he nor his brother could sit down for a week straight. Who thought to set a cow's fart on fire?

She thought back on those first stories sometimes and how much they meant to her. It seemed that Great-Pop was always there to comfort her with a story. He always had something that fit. Even right after Daddy left for good.

Autumn's father had been disappearing for longer and longer after her parents would fight, but he'd always come back before. Then one day he said in a real quiet voice that it was over and he was leaving for good. He asked Autumn if she wanted to come with him, and when she cried that she wanted to stay with Mama, and she wanted him to as well, he told her she wasn't worth his time. Mama changed the locks. It was weird to come home to a house without Daddy, but Autumn handled it pretty well. Until Daddy left the message on their answering machine. He was obviously drunk, and he shouted at the both of them and called them names, and when Autumn was in art class the next afternoon, she started to cry and couldn't stop. Mr. Mikhail, the art teacher, took her out into the hall and tried to talk with her about what was wrong. She liked Mr. Mikhail—he was always nice to her, and he thought that her clay mask showed "real promise." But as he stared at her with his dark, understanding eyes, she suddenly found herself unable to speak, and she began to cry harder. He walked her down to the school nurse.

They called Mama, who called Great-Pop, since he was closest to the school. He drove up in his old Dodge, and she piled herself and her backpack into the front seat.

"You doing okay, princess?" he asked kindly.

She wasn't doing okay at all. Not only was Daddy a jerk, but she'd embarrassed herself in class, and she knew it was going to be all over the school tomorrow. She'd known for a really long time that her parents weren't happy. They'd fought all the time. She couldn't remember the last time they'd hugged. She couldn't remember them smiling. She knew they probably didn't need to be together anymore. Without Daddy in the house, things were a lot quieter too. She didn't have to worry if she was going to say the wrong thing and set him off. But that message from the day before and Mama's reaction to it…. And despite everything, Autumn still missed him. He was still her daddy.

"I-I—" she sobbed, and Great-Pop reached out and squeezed her shoulder. "Don't understand why he left!"

"Autumn," he said, and he chewed on his words for a long time before he spoke them. "You know, honey, sometimes a man can be a *father*, but he's just no good at being a *daddy*."

She continued to sob into her hands, trying to make sense of Great-Pop's words.

"I called him 'Daddy,' but my daddy was no good at being one either," Great-Pop said. "And I didn't understand that there was a difference in fathers until I was a lot older. I thought everyone's was like mine."

The more he spoke in his soothing tones, the more her tears began to slow until she was still crying, but not sobbing. She raised her sopping face and looked at him. "Did your daddy leave too, Great-Pop?"

"In a way," he said quietly.

"Do you hate him?"

"I… just never wanted to be like him," he said. "But I guess I owe him a lot. He made me realize that if I was ever a father, then I wanted to be a better daddy than he was." Great-Pop's voice had grown quiet. "Do you want to hear a story, princess? I want to tell you about the day I decided I wasn't scared about being a father."

CHAPTER 14

THE NEWLYWEDS honeymooned in the barn's hayloft on Roy's family's farm. Roy had offered to take Tommy to a hotel he'd heard about in the city, one that might not mind two men checking in and staying the night together—but that felt too public for Tommy. He just wanted, more than anything, to be alone with the man he'd married.

Their first time happened in the hay. They'd been planning to be together for a while—hinting at it, getting close when they were kissing—but after the exchange of ring for rook, there was no force on earth that could keep them apart. They'd driven back to the farm, hand-in-hand, both anxious, knowing what was about to happen. Neither of them had ever done anything like it before, but when Roy grabbed his new husband and kissed him, Tommy was lost.

"You ready?" Roy asked.

"Hell yes," Tommy said. "You?"

"We could have picked a more romantic spot. And one without an audience, maybe," Roy joked, thumbing over to the trio of grumpy old milk cows that seemed to be watching them. The men were nervous, but excited.

The barn smelled like dust and hay and cows. It was late, and there was no light except for the little lantern Roy had picked up off the shelf near the door. "You sure you don't want me to take you to a bed? Momma's asleep and—"

"No," Tommy insisted. "I think it's perfect here."

Tommy grabbed hold of Roy's shirt, dragging him down into a lingering kiss.

One of the cows let out a long, low moo and turned her face back to her dinner.

Later, when they were spent, Tommy and Roy collapsed back into the hay and held each other and listened to one another's heartbeats and whispered about nothing and everything. In all of his life, Tommy had never experienced anything so fulfilling. He never wanted to move—except if he wanted it to happen again, he was going to have to. He loved Roy more than he'd ever loved anything in his whole life.

Roy traced a light pattern on Tommy's chest and asked, apropos of nothing, "You ever think about kids?" And when Tommy didn't reply, he added, "Like raising 'em?"

It was a tame question; it shouldn't have twisted his gut.

"No," he said in a tight voice.

But that was a lie. He'd thought about it before, and he definitely didn't want them. In Tommy Johnson's opinion, there was nothing at all good that could come from bringing a child into the world—except they were needed to keep things running. Didn't mean that he needed to do his part contributing to the world's population. Wasn't too many years ago that their country had been at war with the whole wide world. What was the point of bringing a child into the world if you were just going to take him right out of it again? And maybe there was some secret he didn't know, but he believed firmly that even if he was selfish enough to put an innocent life into the mess that was their society, he wouldn't be a good father.

"What's wrong?" Roy asked, stroking Tommy's tense muscles with two firm fingers. "You went all weird on me."

"It's just, I don't know much about being a daddy."

"What do you mean? You've got one, don't you?" Roy asked

"Well, yeah. I've got one. But I don't think Daddy likes us all that much, and he definitely never taught me anything about raising kids. How would I teach 'em to be strong? And right? And good?" He was embarrassed to say what he really felt. His daddy had never taught him how to love a child, because he'd never shown an ounce of love himself. "I get the impression we're all sorta in his way. Like maybe he wishes it was just him and Step-Momma now or something."

"He was different when your mama was still alive?"

"Not so much." Tommy shrugged and picked pieces of hay out of Roy's hair. "No, not at all. Guess I've always felt like he hated me."

"Is he mean?"

"Yeah." Tommy nodded. "Yeah, he's mean."

"Least you have one," Roy said after a good long while. "A daddy. I'd give just about anything to have mine back."

Tommy didn't know what to say that wouldn't sound mean and selfish. His daddy was alive and horrible; Roy's was good but dead. Would he trade? He'd certainly have traded his father's life for Roy's father's.

"You think about it, Roy? Kids?"

"Absolutely. I like kids. They're funny."

Tommy turned his head, hay sticking out of his own curls. Hay clung to his sweaty back and poked him too, but he didn't want to get up, didn't want to ever leave this spot. He moved closer to Roy.

"You ever listen to the little kids in church? They think up the most ridiculous things to say, and they have energy that could power the world. You could light up Campbell Springs with a kid-powered generator."

"I reckon you could."

"And sometimes I think I just want to pass on a little bit of me." Roy hadn't even finished his sentence before he put a finger against Tommy's lips. "And none of that 'woe is me, Roy should marry a girl and have babies' horseshit from you, Tom Johnson."

"I wasn't going to say anything." He kissed the tip of Roy's finger.

"Like hell you weren't," he said. "You know, we could be fathers together."

Tommy snorted. "Never mind the mechanics, Roy—I wouldn't want it. I wouldn't know how to be a father. Mine never taught me."

"He did." Roy leaned over and replaced his finger with his lips. When the kiss broke he said, "You just be everything he wasn't. Anything he would do, you do the opposite. You just be you, Tommy. You've got a whole lot to offer a child."

"You think?"

"I know," he said. "I know your heart and your mind and your soul." And with a lecherous grin, he said, "I know your body too now, but that's neither here nor there. The point is, it'd be a really sad world that didn't have at least one child raised by Tommy Johnson. So what do you say? We going to be fathers?"

"I really got to spell out this mechanics business for you?" Tommy laughed. "We can keep on trying, but I'm pretty sure you're not going to get me in a family way, Roy."

"I'm going to go into the orphanage and I'm going to pick me out a son or daughter."

"They aren't just going to let you have one."

"You don't know," Roy said. He really was just teasing now. "I might convince 'em with my vast wealth and social standing." And then, kissing Tommy's collar and neck and jaw, he said, "And then I'm going to give my child to you, and you're going to raise 'em up to be just like you."

"I thought you were going to say you were going to get fifty more and compete with the Campbell Springs Power Company."

"That comes later," Roy said. "That first one though, it's going to have your spirit. I can't wait to meet 'em."

Rolling into his arms, Tommy hugged Roy around the middle and said, "I'm really happy, you know that?"

"I'm glad," Roy answered gently, "'cause it'd be a damned shame if I was the only one grinning like a moron right now."

CHAPTER 15

TOREN ONLY had time to dress in a fresh outfit from the wardrobe down the hall and grab the biggest of the kitchen knives before he saw the sunset light begin to dim outside the window. The sun had not set, though. It still hung low in the sky in exactly the same place it had always been, but gray clouds had moved in, and it began to rain in his Sunset Forest. Toren was far angrier about the violation of his space than he was about Red-Eye's warning. A man ready to fight, Toren charged outside, still damp from his bath. Fat drops of chilled rain soaked into his clean clothing.

"Leave this place!" he shouted through the downpour at a dark figure in the distance. Despite its steady approach, it was not yet close enough for him to make out as man or woman, old or young. Its features were nothing but shadow. "You are not welcome here!"

He brandished the knife, ready to fight the other if need be.

Toren did not expect his challenging cry would deter someone brash enough to come "claim" him, but it still surprised him that his words did not alter the other's pace in the least. The figure did not stop to assess the situation, nor did it hasten to bring the fight to Toren that much more quickly. The stranger moved steadily through the rain, almost casually, its cape—which Toren could also now make out—fluttering behind.

"I will kill you if I have to, to defend my home!"

The man—yes, he was a man—put his hands on the low, flower-covered fence and, with no effort at all, cleared it and kept coming. Toren could see him now in full definition, dressed all in dark clothes. He was young-faced, Toren's age or a little older, with long, dark hair. His blue eyes were clear.

"I'm warning you!" Toren tried again, twisting the knife in his hand.

The stranger wore clothing made of light material but carried a sword at his hip, and from the caddish smirk on his face, he was obviously not afraid of Toren's kitchen knife.

It seemed like cowardice to turn and flee, even though Toren was out-armed. By the time the crow's master had reached him, Toren's entire insides were tightly coiled like a spring. He lunged at the stranger. The other man drew his weapon and disarmed Toren in one clean stroke. Reina's kitchen knife flew through the air, end over end, and then stuck out from the muddy ground where it landed. He stared at it for a second, knowing he'd lose a hand before he reached it. Cowardice or no, without a weapon to defend himself, Toren's instincts made him turn to escape. He was ready to barricade himself in the house, but he found Red-Eye standing behind him, head cocked to the side.

"Toren, my master approaches."

Toren turned back, his jaw clenched in defiance. "If you want my forest, you'll have to kill me."

The caddish smile widened, and the man laughed. "So you're confused. It's understandable—I should have realized. I was a bit confused when I first got here too. Of course I'm not here to kill you. I couldn't if I wanted to…. And you must know, I'd never want to."

"No, I'm not confused. You're in *my* territory thinking you've come to 'claim' me. Your bird said as much." Toren sneered. "Well, I won't be claimed—by anyone!"

At Toren's vehemence, the swordsman's smile slipped just a little. As easily as he'd drawn it, he sheathed his weapon. "Do you know who I am?"

"Rook," Toren said, because the name came to him as vividly as "Toren," "Reina," and "Red-Eye." It wasn't a matter of *knowing* him, because his dark, handsome features were entirely unfamiliar. It was more that he knew the name, as if he'd heard rumors of this man in the past and could identify him by reputation alone.

"Rook," Rook repeated slowly. This seemed to please him a little, and he outwardly cheered up. "At least you remember that much—even if you don't recall that you remember. Well, then, you'll do me the courtesy. Just, who is it that you think you are?"

"You don't know me?" Toren demanded, narrowing his eyes. Rook had journeyed from his domain, trespassing in forest lands that did not belong to him, bringing with him a gray darkness and rain and threats of kidnapping or worse, and he didn't even know who Toren was?

"Oh, I know you," Rook argued easily. Then with a gloved hand he had no business laying on Toren, he took two firm fingers and gently stroked Toren's cheek. "I've known you for a long, long time. I'm just curious if you know yourself."

"My name is Toren," he said, smacking the hand away. Rook studied him for a moment, hand held out where Toren had knocked it, before finally letting it drop down to his side. When Toren spoke, it was on a slow and deliberately cold breath. "And you are on my property, in my forest. Dimming. My. Light."

Rook chuckled, "It's true, I've come for you—you did, after all, ignore my invitation so kindly offered. However, right now I'm concerned about you. You're not—"

"Save your concerns," Toren snapped. "And save whatever right you think it is you have to my person. I'll go nowhere with you."

Rook clucked his tongue. "I was hoping for a different sort of meeting."

Toren glared his opponent down.

"I've waited for you for so very long. But something's not right. This goes beyond confusion." Rook said it as if he were talking to himself, as if Toren weren't standing right in front of him. "And yet." His ice blue eyes lighted on Toren's face. "You and I have a contract, *Toren*. Whether or not you remember. And I did not wait this long only to have you break it."

"Show me where I signed my name," Toren challenged darkly. "Prove it to me. Otherwise, I'm not about to willingly be your slave. You can't take me from my home!"

Toren thought for a moment of his little princess maid and was glad she had gone to whatever place she returned to when she wasn't in the Sunset Forest. He did not know what Rook would do to her if he found her there. Perhaps he would take her in Toren's place and force her to work for him. Would he have come to claim Reina instead? Toren's gaze darkened.

"I'll just have to help you remember your promises," Rook said, all seriousness, and then, "I need you to sleep now, Toren."

Rook motioned to something over Toren's shoulder where the bird stood sentry. He'd forgotten about Red-Eye, but what could one bird do to him besides peck at his skull or eyes? And yet as he turned, ready to catch and throttle the horrible creature that had tormented him, Toren was instead swallowed up in a pair of black wings much, much larger than those of the crow. He twisted in the blackness, clawing at feathers. But the wings were locked there as if clamped by steel, and in that darkness, he lost both strength and consciousness.

"I really wish you had remembered."

There was something in Rook's voice. Tenderness? Wistfulness? Loss? It carried through to Toren from outside the wall of feathers. The last thing Toren remembered was moving his lips to reply when everything went a deeper shade of black.

CHAPTER 16

AUTUMN SHIFTED uncomfortably on the hard pew, careful not to look at her mother or the pastor, for fear of giving herself away.

They were at church for the first time Autumn could remember, because the whole family was there, and they asked Mama if she would join them. Autumn expected Mama to say no. She always did, a little angrily sometimes, when people would insist she join them in their congregation. Privately, she said, "I wish people would keep their religion to themselves and stop trying to shove it down my throat." But this morning, Mama was talking to her brother, and he asked, and she just said, "Yes, we'll be there."

Autumn didn't mind, though she was nervous about going. She didn't know what she was supposed to do, and she didn't know the words or melodies to any of the songs, and she wasn't sure how to say prayers, or if she was going to be asked to speak in front of everyone. But she was a little grateful too, because she thought maybe if they went to church, Jesus and God might see that she was there and listen to her prayers more closely. She'd just sit in the pew and be good and follow along with what everyone else was doing, and maybe when they got out, Mama would get a call that Great-Pop had just opened up his eyes in the hospital, and everything would be all right. It was worth a shot.

But then again, she'd done something bad before she'd come to church. Real bad, and here in this small one-room church with its stained-glass windows and its organist and its loud-talking pastor, maybe Jesus and God would think, *She's worse than that Hannah; don't give her anything she wants.* And she shifted again.

She still couldn't believe she'd done it. Mama had driven her to Uncle Jacob and Aunt Vivian's that morning so she could "formally apologize for running off" at the hospital, even though she'd said a million times that she was sorry when she finally went back to the waiting room. (They never said they were sorry to her for not giving her the time to speak with Great-Pop either, she wanted it noted.) But apparently a million apologies weren't enough for Aunt Vivian, who told her mother all about how *scared* they were and how someone could have just taken off with Autumn—as if she were a six-year-old and not almost a teenager.

So before church, they stopped by the house, and Autumn had to stand in their kitchen and look them both in the eye and apologize for frightening them. Then she had to ask, "Will you please forgive me?"

When everyone was satisfied that she was humiliated enough, she went to the living room and waited, angry at the three of them for being jerks to her. Uncle Jacob poked his head into the living room and said he was sorry for getting upset with her, that she had just scared him was all, and then he went out with the dogs to work on the yard. With Mama and Aunt Vivian talking in the kitchen, Autumn was alone.

Thinking she'd probably get chewed out again if she even turned on the television, she sat there staring at the bookshelf and thinking about nothing and everything. She was still glaring when she saw the gold-leafed spine of the photo album Aunt Vivian had shown her the day before.

It wasn't in her mind to steal the photo when she started turning the pages; she only wanted to look at it again. She wanted to study Great-Pop's face and learn Roy's features too. But when her hand landed on the page, she felt it like a welling pressure behind her eyes. *Get it out, take it; Aunt Vivian doesn't deserve to have this picture.*

Quietly she stood and closed the old wooden door to the living room. She didn't breathe as she moved across the soft, rose-hued carpet. She dimmed the lights, as if the shadows would protect her, and then, with as little noise as she could manage, she peeled back the plastic that covered the photograph. For a long moment she sat there on her knees, holding it in her hand. If Aunt Vivian or Mama came in here, or Uncle Jacob came in from outside, she could pretend she was just studying it closer. She wasn't really going to steal it.

Carefully she flipped over the photograph and looked at the back, expecting Aunt Vivian to have lied to her. But the yellowed paper was blank, she didn't even find Great-Pop's name.

Autumn frowned deeply and flipped the image back over. She felt certain in her heart that this was Roy. His hair wasn't really "long" like Joey Sullivan's, but it was shaggy and hung down into his eyes and over his ears and almost touched his shirt collar. She touched his face. This was the man her Great-Pop had loved and lost. This was the hero in all his stories.

A noise in the house startled her, and she quickly reached into the back of the book where a couple of photos had come loose. Quickly she slapped one on the page where Great-Pop's image had been and then folded the plastic back over it. The new photo was of a woman surrounded by seven children, ranging from babies to elementary school age, but Autumn did not linger on it. She tried to close the album, found that many of the pages had not slid back on the rusted rings, and fumbled with straightening them out before she was able to get the album to lie completely flat. Then she practically flung it back on the shelf, her heart pounding.

She was so caught up in returning the album that she almost left the photograph lying in the middle of the floor. But as the sounds grew closer, she grabbed it off the carpet and leaped with it onto the couch, where she hid it behind one of the cushions. She was just settling in when the living room door opened.

"Autumn?" It was Uncle Jacob. His face was flushed, and he was sweating.

"Yes?" she asked. She could barely swallow, for her heart took up her entire throat.

"Your mama says it's time to get going," he said with a smile.

"Okay," she said, and because she was so nervous, she started lying even though it made her seem even more suspicious. "I was just trying to be quiet in here, so I shut the door. I didn't want to disturb anyone."

He smiled at her. He believed her.

And that was why she wasn't sure God would like her very much anymore, because she had stolen from her family. Even if it was for a good reason, even if it meant she could be that much closer to Great-Pop and understand their secret stories that much better. She carried the photograph with her, tucked deep into her purse. When she was alone, she pulled it out and looked at it, and each time she felt less ashamed about it. (Though it was strange how this fact created its own sense of shame. Why wasn't she ashamed enough? What was wrong with her?)

She wasn't sure what the pastor was talking about. She wasn't listening very carefully. She *tried*, but he read long verses from the Bible, and they kind of bored her. Sometimes, if she concentrated, she understood them, but they didn't mean much to her. She did like one story, which he paraphrased, thankfully, instead of reading. It was about a shepherd who played music to calm down a king who was full of rage. It made her think about music and all the playlists that she and Emma had made together. They had their Dance Mix I, II, III, and III Revisited; there was the Depressio Mix, the Girls Rock! Mix, the Joey Sullivan Mix, and the Best Friends Forever Mix—which she'd deleted once when she and Emma got into a huge fight. Luckily, it blew over, and double luckily, Emma uploaded her copy for Autumn again. She wondered if there was some kind of music she could play for Great-Pop to help him.

She leaned her head back on the pew and stared up at the wooden beams running along the ceiling. A bird stared down at her. It was a black bird, and it cocked its head. She cocked her head back. How did that bird get in here? And was someone going to let it out?

Her mother had just nudged her—it was time to stand and sing another song she didn't know—when she happened to glance out of the corner of her eye and see a young man, a teenager, across the aisle. He was also staring up into the rafters, most likely at her bird. Slowly she slipped up off the hard pew, taking the hymnal her mother had flipped open to the right page for her. But this time she did not even try to sing along. She just kept her eyes on the teenager. He hadn't stood from the pew. He just kept looking at that bird.

But it wasn't *just* that he was being so irreverent—it was *him*. It was his long body and his shaggy black hair, and as his eyes cut across the aisle to her, she saw that they were blue. Bluer than blue. Her breath caught in her throat. He looked just exactly like the man in her photograph, except alive and in color. Without even realizing what she was doing, she reached into her knit purse and pulled it out, right there in church, where God and her family members could see her. And she turned, and she looked again, this time comparing them. There was no mistaking it: it was Roy. Except that just wasn't possible.

It wasn't until the last strains of the song died away that she realized what she'd done, and she hurriedly stuffed the photograph back into her purse.

After the service, her mother muttered, "Did he have to preach about David? Now I've got *Hallelujah* stuck in my head." This didn't make any sense to Autumn as they hadn't sung a song called *Hallelujah*.

"I'll be right back," Autumn promised, and she slipped out of the pew, pushing through the crowd of churchgoers, looking frantically for Roy. Some of the men were the right height, but they weren't the right age, and they didn't have the right face. Her stomach protested the anxiety building in her, but she ignored it. Could he have slipped away?

"Hey, you," a voice nearby said, and she turned, startled to be addressed. It was a younger boy—her own age—but he looked a lot like Roy, with the same dark hair and light blue eyes. "Didja see that bird?"

Her head started to hurt as she stared at him, and her memory flickered. One moment she was looking across the pews at Roy, the next it was this boy, similar but younger, in the seat staring at her. When he smiled, it was rakish, a lot like the photograph, but not exactly the same. His ears weren't right, and his nose was too long. He just looked similar. Could she have mistaken them?

"Were you...?" She felt foolish, ridiculous, but she just had to know. "Were you sitting across from me during the service?"

"You were looking right at me." He laughed like she was an idiot. No, this made a lot more sense. Roy was dead, had been dead for fifty years or more; he wasn't just going to sit down across from her at church. Her mind was tired and stressed and playing tricks on her. She laughed it off, a little too loud and a little too fake.

"Yeah, I guess I was. And yeah, I did see that bird. Wonder how he got in here."

"Not sure." The boy leaned back on his arms against the pew. He smiled with one corner of his mouth and looked her up and down. "Hey, y'know, you're pretty, even if you are kinda short."

Autumn walked back to Mama's side, annoyed.

They got invited for another lunch at another family member's house after church, but Autumn complained loudly about it in the car.

She felt rotten, and she just wanted to go home and go to sleep. Or if Mama insisted on staying out, they should at least go back to the hospital and see Great-Pop.

Her stomach was a mess, and she felt really, really tired all of a sudden. Leaning her head back against the seat, she told her mother she was sick. Mama frowned and reached out with her free hand to feel Autumn's face.

"You're burning up, baby-doll," she declared, a fact Autumn wasn't even aware of, though nonetheless grateful for, as it meant Mama took her straight home.

Dressed down in her pajamas, having refused even the smallest lunch, Autumn climbed up into her big bed with its broad headboard and snuggled into her pink sheets. She laid Great-Pop and Roy's photograph next to her under the pillow. She didn't know about this fever business, but she was very tired. Going to church and trying to be good but being very, very bad and being judged for it was exhausting. It was all she could do to keep her eyes open as Mama tucked the blankets up under her chin.

"When did this come on?" she fretted. Autumn shook her head; she didn't know.

She was almost all the way to sleep, her eyes glazed slits, when she saw him again, this time standing at her bulletin board, which was covered in flowered notes from Emma and photographs of the pair being silly and some cutouts of Joey Sullivan with heart stickers around his head. She was so tired at that point, so close to sleep, that she might have been sleeping and just didn't know it. In any case, she didn't move or start or even call out. She just stared at him.

"Roy," she whispered.

"Hello, princess." His voice wasn't mean, but it wasn't friendly either. Just plain—like the brisk bank teller they always ended up with down at First Bank and Trust when Mama needed to deposit a check.

"It *was* you in church today, wasn't it? Why are you here?" she asked, her eyes closing. She could still hear him in her room, moving around.

"I need something from you."

"Mm." She made a small noise and then said, "Anything. Well, except Great-Pop."

"Princess, that's the problem. We can't both have him."

"But I need him here with me," she mumbled into her pillow.

"Go to sleep now, and I'll tell you a story about how important it is that he come to me, to a place where he can't ever hurt again."

She made another little noise, not agreement or disagreement, just a noise.

"He never told you this because he wanted you to believe in a world that's sweet and good, but princess, if you're old enough to know all about our romancing and such, you're old enough to know what we went through. Tommy—your 'Great-Pop'—had a daddy that was a mean sonofabitch. He liked to drink, and he liked to beat on his kids, and one day, Tommy accidentally gave his Daddy a reason to kill him...."

CHAPTER 17

TOMMY ROLLED over on his back in the hay, straw sticking to his bloodied, tear-streaked face. He was trying not to cry, but the tears were coming hot and fast, despite his best efforts. He'd seen Daddy coming, seen that mean, evil look in his eye, and he hadn't moved quick enough. And Daddy got a hold of him and beat him in the back and the stomach and the face even—when normally he didn't hit where it would show. He hit Tommy so hard and fast that Tommy thought for sure he was trying to kill him this time. Ardeth was screaming from around the corner for him to stop, and that was when Tommy knew why Daddy was upset.

Tommy struggled in his grasp, begging. "It's not true! It's not true, Daddy! I lied! I lied to Ardeth!"

And he could hear his younger sister crying and saying she was sorry she'd told; she was so, so sorry. She begged Daddy to stop hurting Tommy.

But Daddy had no room in his hateful heart for Ardeth's pleas, and Tommy recanting only seemed to make him angrier. Tommy's nose was gushing blood now, which probably saved his life; Daddy went to grab his face and couldn't get a good grip for all the slick blood. That's when Tommy found an out, twisted away from his father, and started to run.

He flew out the screen door, down the rotting steps, and fled across their lawn. He didn't look back until he was well past the lake— almost twenty minutes away. He couldn't breathe, and his side and throat burned with the effort of his escape. He stumbled, dirt pluming around him as he fell. Sweat and blood dripped on the road.

He couldn't find the barn until almost nightfall, and by that point, he was so tired he would have slept on the ground if it meant he could just stop moving. The hay was dry and warm, and as he collapsed into it, the tears came. Not because Daddy hated him; Daddy had always hated him, but because Ardeth had told.

He covered his eyes with his arm and tried to quiet his tears. He wished Roy were here to hold him. He hoped Roy wouldn't go by the house, though he was certain as long as Daddy didn't have his gun, Roy could take him. Horrible flashes of Roy beating his father's head in with a brick did nothing to still the deep pain in his heart over Ardeth's betrayal.

He couldn't say for certain why he'd told her, except that he loved her the best out of all of his siblings, and because she had a friendly and forward way of thinking. So while they were fishing the day before yesterday, he'd just said it, plain as he could muster.

"Ardeth, I'm in love."

"You are?" she asked excitedly. He knew she wasn't going to be too pleased that she wouldn't be standing as a bridesmaid in some fancy church wedding, but he really didn't anticipate just how disappointed his admission would make her. "With who?"

"Roy."

She blinked for a long second, her smile hovering awkwardly before it started to fade. "Roy McMillan? From church?"

"Yes," he said, already beginning to regret his decision.

"He's... a... *he*." She started to laugh a little, tugging on her line and turning away from him. "You've got a weird sense of humor, brother."

"I'm not joking."

"So what are you saying then?" she asked, anger blooming on her cheeks. "That you're some kinda flit?"

He chewed the inside of his lip. He could still laugh it all off, but the rook in his pocket weighed heavy. He just wanted someone to know. Someone he cared about. He swallowed and nodded. "I guess. I don't think about it like that. I just... know I love Roy."

Ardeth stood abruptly, letting her fishing pole fall back on the bank. "I wish you would take it back." She was stiff and awkward. "I don't like it, Tommy, I wish you would take it back."

"I can't take it back, Ardeth." He shook his head. "Then I would be lying to you. And I can't lie to you because you're—" *My favorite,* he didn't get to say. She started off without him, her long ponytail waving back and forth as she shook her head.

The next night at dinner, she wouldn't look at him, but she didn't say anything about it either, and no one else seemed to notice anything was amiss. He was hurt that his little sister was disgusted with him, but there was a part of him that didn't regret telling her. He hoped—even if it was a far-off and foolish hope—that she would remember he was her favorite too. And she would forgive him for falling in love with a man. Or love him in spite of it.

He never in a million years would have dreamed she would tell Daddy. Maybe she hadn't. Maybe she'd told Step-Momma or his brother or a friend of hers, he didn't know, but somehow it had gotten back to Daddy and made Daddy want to kill him.

The night after the beating, Tommy had terrible nightmares, and he woke up more than once, screaming in the empty barn. In the dreams, Ardeth was riding on Daddy's back like she did when she was just a little girl, and she was saying, "Faster! Faster! Hit 'im harder, Daddy, he's still moving!"

He set out for Roy's before dawn and found him in the barn milking the cows. He was singing to himself. Any other day, Tommy would have stood and listened and made fun of him or joined in. Today, though, he ran to Roy and threw his arms around his back while he knelt in the hay.

"Tommy," Roy said warmly, thinking it was an early morning surprise, and that Tommy had come to make love with him in the loft. He smiled until he felt Tommy's body shaking against his back, and then he untangled himself, and turned and saw Tommy's bruised and broken face. Tommy had told Roy about his father many times before, so he knew without a second thought who had done it.

"You should go in the house and let Momma clean you up," Roy told him in a voice that lacked color. Tommy thought again about Roy bashing his father's head in with a brick, and there were parts of him that wanted it so very, very much. But if Roy killed Daddy, it wouldn't undo what Ardeth had done, and he didn't want anyone to lay a finger on his sister—even if she had broken his heart.

"Don't go over there," he begged. "I know what you're thinking."

Tenderly Roy kissed the only part of Tommy's face that wasn't swollen.

"I'm sorry, but that just isn't possible. The devil himself would be scathed by what I'm thinking right now. You need to go inside to Momma and let her clean you up."

"You do anything and the police will take you away from me."

"Go inside, Tommy. Let me handle what needs handling."

Roy's mother was a gentle woman with sad eyes. He always felt like she knew everything about the two of them, but she never said a word. That morning, she heated up water on the stove and got out her softest rag and took to cleaning up his face, dabbing his cuts with iodine. It had been a long time since he felt the tenderness of a mother's hand, his own having died when he was still young. Step-Momma wasn't the tender sort, and she was kind of stupid about things like first aid. He wouldn't have wanted her coming at his face with anything that stung.

After Roy's momma had cleaned him up, she drew a bath for him and poured Epsom salts in the bottom of the tub. He soaked for a long time and tried not to think about Daddy with his gun or the sheriff hauling Roy away. They should just leave town. Pack their things—or Roy's things rather, as he didn't think he'd ever get anywhere near his house again—and climb into the truck and start driving. They should go out West. Things were better out there. Things were better anywhere but here.

Roy didn't come home until midday, but when he did, he went straight for his room where his mother had set Tommy up on the bed with many blankets and pillows. She was treating him like he was sick rather than injured, but he was so moved by her tenderness that he just drank it in. He even let her help him into a pair of Roy's pajamas, which were much too long for him.

"Mind if I join you?" Roy asked quietly, slipping off his work shirt.

He didn't seem at all worse for wear. There wasn't a speck of blood on him anywhere, and Tommy wondered if maybe he hadn't just driven around until he cooled down. Even so, Roy stopped to take some of his headache powders, downing the whole packet without water. While Roy was grimacing at the taste, Tommy took his opportunity to express his concerns.

"Your mother might not like it if she found you in bed with me."

Tommy wanted nothing more in the whole world than for Roy to climb up beside him, but hadn't he just taken a world of a beating for not being more cautious?

Roy quietly locked his door with a key that was hanging on a hook.

"Don't worry, I'm not going to sully your good name. I really do just want to sleep."

"Well, in that case." And he made room for Roy on the bed and eased into him as he felt his husband's arms wrap around him. There was so much pain, but Roy made it just a little better by lying close.

It was about three days before the news that Tommy's father had gone missing reached the McMillan farmhouse. Roy's mother told them at breakfast after they'd finished the morning chores. She looked worried, overestimating Tommy's reaction. But Tommy's only concern was for Roy, who swore on his grave—but not Tommy's—that he had nothing in the world to do with it.

CHAPTER 18

TOREN'S EYES opened on the rain-bearing sky. For a moment he only
stared, sleep-confused, and wondered why none of the droplets were
hitting him in the face when he could see and hear them falling. And
then, as the fog faded, he realized there was a small round hole in the
roof, big enough to let in rain, and that above his sheer-curtained bed
was a glass awning that tapered into six distinct spouts. The rain that
fell from the sky splattered the clear covering, tapping like fingers
against the surface. It then trailed down, pooling into spouts, where it
created little fountains that fell gracefully into six shallow pools in the
floor. The sight of it touched him so deeply it made his heart ache.

He sat up in the warm, dry bed, the moon-blue covers falling
down his chest, and listened to the gentle patter of the rain above him
and the rainwater trickling down into the pools.

The walls were gray stone, and the windows placed at even
intervals could be unlatched and opened outward, revealing more rain
beyond. The largest of the windows cast colorful shadows on the floor
as the weak sunlight strained through a stained-glass image of a purple
butterfly on a tree branch. For a moment he let the peace and beauty
permeate his mind.

But Toren had not forgotten anything.

He awoke, still companions with all his strange memories of the
day before. He knew exactly who he was and exactly where he was *not*.
He was not at home in his comfortable and rustic Sunset Cottage. Nor
was he bathing in the endless, golden light.

He was in Rook's domain, forcibly brought here by the fiend and
his bird.

His thoughts turned to escape.

But even if he'd known where to acquire a weapon, an ill-timed
sense of modesty prevented him from vacating the bed. His clothes were

nowhere to be seen, and he lay completely naked on the firm mattress. He tried not to think about who had undressed him, but he couldn't help that a flash of Rook's large hands peeling his wet clothing off, revealing naked flesh, went through his mind. That damned cad!

Toren was just considering fashioning a makeshift covering out of the sheets when a trapdoor in the floor opened upward. Slowly a woman ascended the steps carrying a silver tray laden with food. She did not trail gold dust.

She was tall and handsome, with long, feathery black hair and dark eyes. Well, a single dark eye at least; the other was hidden behind an eye patch. He knew at once who she was, and he narrowed his eyes.

"So you can take human form?"

That was how she'd been able to wrap him up in her wings—she was almost as tall as he was.

Red-Eye cocked her head to one side.

"My master sends food, Toren."

As sullen and obstinate as Toren felt, the food looked very good, and the aromas drifted around him and seduced his nostrils. He allowed her to lay the tray in his lap without much protest. There was a fruit bowl full of oranges, grapes, pears, and peaches, a small loaf of steaming white bread, an array of cheeses, and chicken, beef, pork and lamb skewers. It was a tiny feast, neatly and attractively arranged for him on the silver tray. He scooped food up with both hands and shoveled it into his mouth. If his captor meant to poison him, he would go willingly, ravenously, to his death. He was on his fourth skewer of meat when he noticed Red-Eye had not moved but was still standing there, her sharp chin jutted out, watching him eat.

"What?" he demanded. He wanted her gone so he could eat and plot out his escape in peace.

"My master hopes that this food will please you."

The food did please him—greatly—but he wasn't about to give Rook the satisfaction of knowing that. He shrugged one shoulder and said instead, "You know what would please me more, crow? Being allowed to return to my home."

She stared at him quietly and then said, "Why are you not pleased to be claimed by my master?"

He blinked, disbelief rising inside of him. Had she really just asked why he was not *pleased* to be kidnapped and taken from his forest home? Why he was not *pleased* to trade golden sunlight for rain? Why he was not *pleased* to find himself defenseless and naked in this strange place?

"You can tell him the food is fine," he finally managed.

Red-Eye was silent for a good minute before she finally said, "When you've eaten, my master wishes for you to join him in his bedchamber."

His imagination again turned to Rook undressing him. He tried to focus. Tried to convince himself that it was the bird woman who had removed his clothing.

"And what if I mean to leave this place?"

She continued to stare at him with what was becoming a familiar non-answer and then asked, "Why do you want to leave? My master wants you."

Toren sighed heavily and said, "Bring me my clothes and I will meet with him. But certainly *not* in his bedchamber."

Red-Eye obliged with a nod and disappeared back down the hatch. In that moment, Toren shoved the tray aside and leaped from the bed, yanking the covers off the mattress. He twisted them around his body. Once he was out in the rain, they would be useless, as good at covering him as tissue, but for this moment at least, he could hide himself.

He then hurried to one of the open windows and looked out, but the drop was substantial with nothing there to break his fall. He must be at least three floors up, and while the castle wall was made of thick stones with handholds that he could have attempted to climb down, they were as slick as the rocks at the waterfall. If he fell from this height, it would not be soft creek muck that he landed in but hard ground. No, the hatch was his only option and he moved silently to it, hoping she had not locked it from underneath.

Relief filled him as the trapdoor gave. Not locked. Not guarded. The stairs underneath were shadowed and silent, and Toren hesitated only for a moment before he began to descend. If Red-Eye was quick with his clothing, he might have to hurt her to get past—something he was not keen to do, despite how much she frustrated him.

He held up the sheet like a trailing train and moved stealthily in his bare feet, down a seemingly endless spiral staircase. When it finally opened up at a doorway, Toren fell back against the wall, his heart pounding in protest. If by some miracle he escaped this realm, where was he going to go? Rook would certainly return for him if he made his way back to the Sunset Cottage. What lay beyond the rain and the sunset? Should he travel on elsewhere, exploring these lands in nothing but a wet sheet? The prospect was less than appealing.

Quickly he glanced out beyond the doorframe and saw an extravagant entrance hall with a vaulted ceiling and sweeping stairway, illuminated on both sides by inset candles. At the first landing where both sides of the blue-carpeted staircase joined, there was a large picture window made, seemingly, of a single piece of crystal-clear glass. It looked out on hillocks dotted with trees. The sky was heavily overcast, pierced by long fingers of gray-white light which cut out of the clouds like they meant to stroke the hills in a loving caress. The sight of it drew Toren forward, stupidly, from his hiding space, and he was momentarily oblivious to his exposure. It was not until he heard the smug voice behind him that he realized all his sneaking had been for naught.

"An interesting wardrobe choice," Rook said. "I thought you might like to have your wet clothes laundered, but I see you're not so picky."

Toren turned, embarrassed with himself for losing sight of what he was doing as he looked out over the lands. He said the first thing that came to mind.

"I've no desire to join you in your bedchamber."

Rook contemplated this. "So you still don't remember, then?"

"Remember?" Toren scoffed. "I'm sure whatever memories have been taken from me will have no bearing on whether or not I submit my body to the will of a kidnapper."

"So it doesn't concern you that I'm a man, only that you think me a rakehell?"

"Something like that," Toren said tightly, pressing his lips together.

"I've no intention of forcing you." He said this with such a devious smile that Toren shied away just a little. "I'm offering you something, Toren. I'm offering you the return of your memories."

"In exchange for giving myself to you?"

"Crudely put, but yes, I suppose."

"So you have them, then? My memories, and you could return them freely, but instead you want me to pay for them. You want my body as an exchange?"

Rook was slow as he moved forward, and Toren, remembering his moment of cowardice when he turned to flee at the Sunset Cottage, stood rooted firmly to the spot. He would not show weakness here.

"How is this not force disguised as trade?" Toren demanded as Rook rounded him, taking his time, looking Toren over. He stopped beside him, and Rook's fingers grazed Toren's side as he reached out and tugged up the edge of the sheet where it had slipped.

"Got to cover your modesty," Rook said with slow sarcasm. He let his fingers linger there, hot little pressure points on Toren's skin that took Toren's voice away from him.

"You're going to have to forgive me, Toren. It's just—" He breathed and leaned to kiss Toren's jaw. His lingering lips set every nerve ending abuzz, and Toren almost gave in to the kiss. It was gentle, not at all ravenous as he'd expected. "—been so very long."

Rook inhaled Toren's scent and pulled back. And though there was now space between them, it took Toren a moment before he had complete control over his own body.

"Once you remember yourself, I can assure you that you will not be worried about things like fair trade. Once you remember, you'll willingly—eagerly even—want to join me in my bed." With a wicked smile he added, "We'll see if I still let you, after the chilly welcome I've received."

Toren snorted hotly, "You're so certain. Give me my memories then. If you're right, then you'll get what you want anyway. If you aren't, then you've done me a good turn and I'll thank you—just not with my body."

Rook raised one dark eyebrow.

"I'm appealing to your sense of reason as a man who… has a history with me?"

Rook considered this for a long moment before he nodded. "Of course." And then, "Yes, of course. I would absolutely gift your memories to you and send you home if I could. It's really not as appealing as one would imagine to have you here when you don't even know who I really am. But I'm afraid it just doesn't work that way."

Toren scoffed incredulously.

"I *would* just give you your memories," Rook assured him. "But I don't know how."

Toren was taken aback by what seemed like honesty and some distant relative to vulnerability in Rook's voice. Rook reached out and touched him again, this time on the shoulder. Toren could have moved. He chose not to.

"I believe that if we're joined, bodily, you will remember me. And if you remember me, *Toren*"—he heavily emphasized the name—"you will want to be joined with me bodily."

"I...." Toren shook his head. How silly they seemed, having this conversation out in the grand hall, while he was wearing nothing but a sheet. And if Rook didn't stop touching him, the sheet, which did a passable job at hiding his modesty, would not be hiding much of anything at all. "I need to think."

"All right."

"And I need to send word to my princess maid that I am here with you, and she isn't to worry."

This did not seem to please Rook in the least. "I fear she may be part of the problem."

"She's not," Toren replied firmly. He couldn't imagine a world in which Princess Reina was a problem for anyone.

"She doesn't *belong* here. I think it best you have no more contact with her."

"Is that so?" Toren asked, tilting his chin proudly. "Well, I think that if you keep my princess from me, there is no chance I will ever, *ever* submit to you. Memories or no."

"Would you reward me if I brought her here?" Rook asked after considering Toren's threat for what seemed like forever.

"Not necessarily. Not in *that* way at least."

"What if payment were something simpler? Easily given. What if you didn't have to move from this spot?"

Toren raised an eyebrow.

Rook laughed at his expression. "Surely a single kiss is worth your precious princess maid?"

Toren sighed, "I don't see how—"

But Rook had no interest in waiting for permission. He'd come forward, snaking his arms around Toren's sheet-covered waist and pulling him hard against his body. "It's just a kiss," Rook breathed before he put his lips against Toren's. Should he protest? *Had* he protested? Toren couldn't remember. In that moment there was nothing but Rook's firm lips, gently teasing his own apart. Toren kissed back, tasting the other man, sucking at his bottom lip. Rook's mouth was intoxicating, and quite suddenly, Toren forgot why he ever resisted. He *liked* kissing Rook. But after only an appetizer's worth of his mouth, Rook pulled away. The sensation of their mouths pressed together lingered, and Toren was dumb with the moment. Lost in it. Uncertain what they'd even been talking about.

"Do you remember me now?" Rook asked.

"Mmn," Toren agreed, warmth lingering on his lips. "Rook."

Silence was his reply. The arms around his waist fell away, leaving him feeling cold.

Toren slowly opened his eyes to find he was standing alone, clutching his sheet, as Rook walked away from him toward the staircase.

"Allow my servant to dress you, and we will go *visit* your Sunset Forest." The way he emphasized the word left no room for doubt. Rook did not consider it Toren's home, and if Toren was wise, he would begin to make himself comfortable in the Rain Kingdom.

CHAPTER 19

AT TEN to three, Autumn dragged herself out of her own bed and climbed up into Mama's. Her nightgown was a wrinkled, sweaty mess, but it was too much effort to go back to her wardrobe and find something else to wear. She was too old to be sleeping in Mama's bed, but her mother welcomed her with open arms and let her snuggle up against her side while she watched television on a really low volume. It felt nice, and Mama's bare leg was cool against Autumn's burning skin.

She had the sense that Roy had followed her into the bedroom, but Mama didn't say anything about it. Maybe she couldn't see him? Autumn didn't like Roy's stories as much as Great-Pop's. For one thing, he told them matter-of-factly, unadorned with the details that made her favorite stories so interesting. For another, his were sad. Not as sad as the one Great-Pop told her. Her least favorite story. But sad enough to weasel their way into her heart and sit there heavily. The only thing she appreciated about it was just how much Roy loved Great-Pop and how willing he was to defend him against his awful father. He hadn't said specifics, but she hoped whatever he'd done to Great-Pop's daddy, it hurt real bad.

"Mama?" Autumn moaned against her mother's side. Her mouth was dry and her stomach ached.

"Hold on just a second," Mama whispered, and Autumn realized she'd been talking on the phone. Had she dozed off again? "Yes, baby-doll?"

"I don't want Great-Pop to…." As soon as she began to talk, she felt like it was too much effort, and she started fading again. Snuggling deeper against Mama's leg, she pulled the covers up over her head. For a moment, there was silence as Mama waited for her to continue, but as Autumn's breathing evened, she addressed her caller again.

"Sorry about that, she's burning up, poor thing. It just came out of nowhere. Maybe stress. I shouldn't have pulled her out of school." She paused. "I know, I just didn't *think,* and you were busy... I just couldn't go there alone." She let out a long, low sigh, "I'm a shit mother. No, I really, really am. She's been an absolute wreck about all of this." Another long pause in which Autumn almost fell asleep. "Yeah. Well. She just loves Granddad like nothing I've ever seen." For a long time she just listened, and then Mama laughed. "Well, she's always been a special heart. I don't remember loving my Great-Gramps like that. But then I was a real brat. And he was weird, and he was old, and I just wasn't very interested. You had a weird Grandpa, didn't you?"

Mama's words were coming to her through a thick haze of sleep, so they were slightly distorted, and not all of them made sense. She could be dreaming again. She shifted just a little.

"She's talking about Virginia's father." Roy was sitting on the floor, his arm up on the mattress near where Autumn was lying. She could see him through a crack in the covers, but he wasn't looking at her. He was staring straight ahead. "Do you want to hear about how Tommy and Virginia came to be married when he loved me so much?"

"You died," Autumn told him, figuring that was the long and short of it. People died, and people moved on.

"What, baby-doll?" Mama asked and felt under the covers for her, placing a tender hand on her back. "Hey, Jack? Can I call you later? I think she really needs... yeah.... Okay, thanks, baby." Her voice dropped to an almost inaudible level. "Love you too."

"I did die," Roy agreed. "And for about five years, it was like your Great-Pop had died too. He was all alone. And then he met Virginia Stewart, at church of all places. And he fell in a certain kind of love with her. Do you understand? Not the same sort of love we'd felt for each other, but a companionable fondness. A friendship really. She was older than he was and a widow, and she had seven children."

"Tell me," Autumn insisted, unable to open her eyes.

VIRGINIA AND Tom sat out on the little concrete patio in front of their church. No one was around—just the two of them. It was their Saturday to rake the leaves off the front lawn. Now, the task completed, Virginia had made some lemonade in the small church kitchen, and they sat close together, drinking it.

In the summer the congregation held barbeques on the mowed lawn beyond the building, and the kids ran and played and climbed all over the poor gazebo, which was only a season or two from falling completely down. But summer had gone, taking with it all the warmth and sunshine for the year. It was now a chilly autumn. Most of the trees had lost their leaves, but the ones that still had foliage were bursting with vibrant colors.

"It looks like a sunset," Virginia said about the rich yellows and red and oranges. She had a quiet and polite way about her, and the things she said were kind. Even when she was tending a fussy baby or reprimanding an overly eager eight-year-old, she went about all things with kindness. It was one of the reasons Tom liked her so much.

"Does," Tom agreed with a sad little nod. Autumn was the hardest time of the year for him and sundown the hardest time of the day. Spring was hardest on Virginia.

She reached out and offered him her gloved hand, which he took silently. She'd knitted the gloves herself and the yarn was baby soft. He relaxed just a little in their companionable embrace. Looking back on that moment, he believed it was her little hand on his that had made him decide. He didn't even have a ring yet. "Virginia?"

"Yes, Tom?" she asked.

"I would like to marry you."

Her fingers sprang open as if his skin had burned her through the gloves, but he turned and gave her a steady look. Surprise etched every inch of her lovely face, and she shook her head.

"You're fooling me," she said.

"No, I'm not. I'd like to marry you, and if you would like and they would like, I'd be something like a father to your children. Not their daddy, of course, I wouldn't suppose that, but a man in the house." Slowly he turned his eyes back to the line of trees jacketed in fall colors. "I've been thinking about this for a long time. I hope you'll say yes."

"Tom?" she asked quietly, "Do you love me?"

"You know that I do," he said.

"But you aren't *in love* with me, are you?" She was such a beautiful woman with such a gentle heart. Any other man would be lucky to find himself in love with her.

He squeezed her hand, which he had not released, and slowly her fingers curled back around into their comfortable grip.

"No, I'm not."

For a long time there was only the sound of the October wind sweeping behind the building.

"Virginia Stewart, you deserve a man who will be in love with you, body and soul. I love your heart and your mind and your gentle way. And I love the time we spend together. You are the best friend I've had… in a long time. But I can't be a man who will be in love with you, body and soul. Do you understand?"

"Maybe."

"I'm already in love that way, with someone else. And to let myself love like that, to let someone take their place, would be to betray a vow I made. But if you agree to marry me, you will find in me a true friend and the best father I know how to be. I'll provide for you and your children, and I will always be true to our marriage, and Virginia, if you meet someone else, and he will love you in the way you really deserve, the way I can't, then I'll do anything you want."

Virginia had started to silently cry, the flipped up ends of her bouffant bobbing.

"I'm sorry," Tom said. "I'm not being fair to you."

She turned glistening eyes on him. "Tom," she whispered, and she threw her arms around his shoulders. "I would love to marry you."

They kissed then, gently and without romance. It was the same kiss they would share later in the month when they went before the justice of the peace and said their vows, Tom in his simple suit, Virginia in her Sunday dress.

"Will you tell me about her now?" Virginia asked, so low that the wind almost completely swallowed up her words.

Tom shook his head, leaning into her. "I can't tell you everything. It would feel like betrayal." But knowing that he was going to spend the rest of his life with this woman, he figured he should try to trust her at least with the most basic part. "I'll tell you one thing, and that's all I can share with you, Virginia."

"All right."

"And if I say it and you don't want to marry me anymore, I won't be put out with you. But there's one more thing: you have to make a promise."

"Of course," she agreed. Virginia was not a woman prone to flights of fancy, but she seemed almost breathless at the prospect of finally hearing about Tom's wife. They shared this sadness—the loss of someone they had loved profoundly, but where she found great solace in talking about Charlie and how hard it was waking up in their bed alone, Tom kept the specifics of his loss locked up very tight in his chest. It was a rare thing, letting her into this sacred place.

"This promise, Virginia, I'd sooner have you break our wedding vows than break this promise to me."

"I understand," she agreed again, a little more solemnly. She put her free hand on his shoulder. "Tom, I promise."

"I need you to never reveal to the children that ours isn't a marriage of lovers."

She nodded sadly. "I wouldn't."

"And I need you to promise that you will never tell them about… my spouse."

She hesitated for a moment, then nodded, one short, heavy nod.

"The person I lost, the one I loved with every part of me, my most important person? His name was Roy." Tom breathed out the words; in his mind Ardeth was right there beside him, looking disgusted. He didn't look at Virginia as he said any of this. He wasn't expecting much, or perhaps he was expecting everything. If his own sister—whom he had not spoken to since that night—had not stood by him, then how could he expect this woman, who wasn't even his blood, to stand by him? After all, she was a good, churchgoing lady. And this sort of thing disgusted good, churchgoing ladies.

"There are so many things I want to ask you right now, Tom," Virginia said after only a moment's pause. "But I won't pry." And then she laid her head against his arm and said, "Thank you for being my friend."

CHAPTER 20

REINA BLINKED. Her lovely lace sleeves were rolled up to her elbows, and her arms were deep in warm, sudsy water. Her reflection stared back at her from the murky depths of the bucket, broken in the froth. How had she come to be standing here? She couldn't quite remember, and she couldn't remember anything before this moment either, except the other time she'd found herself in the little bed in the closet. She remembered that vividly.

Thinking there was nothing for it, she pulled out two rags from the bucket and started to scrub the caked mud prints on the hardwood floor. Toren had been tramping through the forest—this much she was certain of. She smiled as she thought of him, warmed inexplicably. As far as she knew, she'd only ever just met him the day or week or month before. Time really had very little meaning to her here.

For hours she worked, moving forward by degrees until she had scrubbed the entire entrance hall, and her bucket was a swampy brown. Then, wiping sweat out from under her circlet, she stood and hauled the whole mess to the sink in the kitchen where she carefully poured it down the drain. There was still more mud to scrub. She'd found it trailed up the stairs and into the bathroom where even the tub was ringed with the dirt Toren left behind. But feeling a break was in order, Reina sat down for a moment at the kitchen table and stared out the window at the sunset.

She still felt it, that sense that *here* was not her real home, but she enjoyed herself regardless. In the Sunset Cottage, she could let her mind drift, or she could turn it off completely if she wanted.

When Reina felt she could not possibly justify laziness any longer, she prepared dinner for herself and Toren, peeling potatoes and chopping carrots and onions and a pumpkin that she'd gathered from the garden out back. She unwrapped a thick slice of red meat, which she had found in the icebox under the stairs, and cut the flesh into workable bites. Then she floured it and browned it and put the whole thing into a pot that was almost as large as she was and set it simmering. Soon the entire kitchen was filled with the smell of stewing meat and vegetables. It was going to be a delicious dinner, and Toren would be very pleased.

Reina finished cleaning the stairs next, which took considerably less time than the whole of the entryway, and then made short work of the hallway and the bathroom. All the while her belly was grumbling as the smells began to permeate the whole household. When she had cleaned all there was to clean, she went outside and played on the swing near the back of the house, waiting for her dinner to finish and her friend to return. Perhaps it wasn't very becoming of a princess to swing, but then she remembered that she was a princess who did housework in a forest where the sun never set, and things like propriety really didn't much matter.

She had just gained height when she saw them approaching. She was on a backswing, her skirts flying forward, when she called out happily and waved to Toren. By the time she'd swung forward again, however, she could feel something greater than gravity dragging her down to the ground.

Toren walked stiffly beside his traveling companion, whom she recognized but also didn't recognize at all. His features made her head hurt, and she reached for her suddenly throbbing right temple as she swung still higher. Her braid flew behind her, a wild rope which snapped when she changed direction. Flower petals fell from her hair to the ground. She caught the hard earth with the heels of her boots, dragging long marks into the dirt as she slowed, her skirts finally coming to a stop around her.

She could not remember him exactly, and yet she knew him. Knew him extremely well. And then Toren too, seemed suddenly more familiar. As if she'd known him in a context far beyond this present moment.

"Toren?" she called, trying to keep the worry from her voice. She wanted to call him something else, like Toren was the wrong name, or she hadn't pronounced it correctly. But there was nothing else there. Even when she wracked her brain, she couldn't think of what other name there might be. She tried not to run to him, but a strange sort of fear gripped her. She needed, quite desperately, to get him away from the dark-haired man who was walking beside him. "Toren, I'm so glad you're back!" It was hard to keep her voice light and airy. "I've made dinner for us. I...." Etiquette battled her feelings of fear and distrust for the stranger. "I'm sorry," she addressed the man whose name dangled on the tip of her tongue, "but I haven't made enough for us all. Perhaps you'll join us for dinner another time."

He blinked cold blue eyes at her, and she knew he saw through her lie. There was enough stew to feed five more at least.

"Fine," he said. "My servants will have dinner waiting for us when we return anyway."

"Us?" she repeated slowly.

"Toren and I," he informed her.

"And you, Princess Reina, if you want," Toren insisted with a tight smile. She looked from the man she felt such intense warmth for to the man she so instantly disliked. He was staring at her plainly, and nothing in his features betrayed the slightest hint that he wished she would join them. "I've come to let you know that I will be staying with Rook for a while."

Rook.

Rook? Was that his name? Rook? It didn't fit exactly. It was as if the corner stuck up just a bit, and it could be peeled back to reveal another name.

She glared at *Rook*. "Toren is having dinner with me. I've gone to a lot of trouble to clean up the house and to prepare our food."

"Is that so?" Rook replied mildly.

"That's so," she fired back, tilting her little chin.

Rook turned to Toren as if she had not said anything at all and whispered something into his ear. This sent Toren's normally defiant gaze sideways. He nodded, dejected.

"Reina, I... I'm sorry about dinner, princess. Could you store the leftovers for me?"

"You *want* to go back with him? I don't understand, Toren! This is our Sunset Forest. Aren't you happy here with me?"

"Yes!" he exclaimed. "Yes, yes, absolutely. I'm the happiest here with you."

Rook raised an eyebrow warningly.

"But there's something I need to do."

"No," Reina said defiantly. "If you go with him, you're going to... forget me." She didn't know why she said it.

"He won't forget you," Rook said coldly. "You just won't have the hold over him that you do now."

"I'm not holding him anywhere! I wouldn't! Please, Toren, please don't go with him. I don't know how or why, but he'll do very bad things to you."

"Funny," Rook told her, "I've said exactly the same thing about you." And then he reminded Toren, "You've told her where you'll be. The stew seems important to her, so I vote she should stay here and tend to it. You and I will return to the castle without her."

For a long moment Reina looked around the blooming garden. She could feel the sun on the back of her neck, and she fingered the braid that hung over her shoulder. She did not want to leave this place. She felt warm and special here. There was nothing waiting for her beyond the forest... except Toren.

"I'm invited?" she asked loudly, looking right at Rook as she did.

"*Toren* has invited you."

"Then I'll go," she said, "and I will cook Toren's meals, and I will clean his rooms, and I will keep him company."

"Princess." Toren smiled, obviously relieved.

"If you come, then you will sit on the throne like a proper princess, and you will not lift a finger to help him."

"That's punishment!"

"He cares for you and wants you nearby, and I care for him and want him nearby, so I can't rid myself of you without darkening his heart further to me. But that doesn't mean I'll allow you free access to him."

"But you can't keep her prisoner," Toren said.

"No one said she will be a prisoner. She's a princess, remember? She should act like one. No more cleaning, no more swings, no more stew-making. Being royalty means lessons and court and fittings and balls. It means responsibility. When she is not busy with any of the other duties that the kingdom requires of her, *then* you can see her. Those are my terms." He shrugged. "Otherwise she can stay here and continue to scrub floors in an empty house. The two of you make your decision quickly."

Princess Reina ran to Toren, and he wrapped her in a warm hug.

"I don't want you to go back with him!" she begged.

He bent down and whispered into her ear. "Come with us."

"But I don't want to sit on the throne. I'm a princess who's also a housekeeper, remember?"

"If you stay here, we won't see each other again."

"You can escape!"

"He's offered me my memories back."

"You don't need them, Toren!" she cried, loud enough for Rook to hear—though maybe he could hear everything anyway. "I don't have mine, and we're fine that way. You mean everything to me. I can't say why, but even though I don't know you, I *know* you. You're...." Again, his name stuck in her throat, like it wasn't quite right. He responded to it with a smile. "But if you get your memories back, maybe...."

Maybe he wouldn't need her anymore.

"You won't have to spend *every* second on the throne," he reminded her, bopping her chin with his pointer finger. "Don't you have a home to go to?"

Home. Yes. That was right. There was still that "somewhere else" she had to return to sometimes. She blinked slowly. It was so warm here, so pretty, so safe, so nice, that "Home" no longer seemed as important to her.

"You won't let him keep us apart?" she pleaded.

"Ten seconds," Rook warned, and both the child princess and the handsome blond man cast him a withering look. He laughed, waving off their mutual intensity. "Make your decision. We're leaving."

"I won't let him keep us apart," Toren promised. "Get something to carry your stew. We'll eat it together at the castle."

CHAPTER 21

AUTUMN WAS still not feeling any better on Monday, and Mama called their neighbor, Miss Juanita, and asked if she could please come and sit with her. Miss Juanita agreed enthusiastically. She seemed to like Autumn, but more importantly, she enjoyed their large television set. She said it was much easier to follow her stories on 32 inches of HD television than on the old tube TV with the manual dial she'd inherited from her mother. Miss Juanita was a good caretaker, and Mama trusted her.

Autumn didn't care either way; she could barely keep her eyes open. When she did wake up, she was often confused about where she was and what was going on. She was having strange dreams that bled through into her waking moments. One time she opened her eyes, sweating in her thin nightgown, certain she was dressed in a full gown with bodice and multiple layers under her skirts. It took her a moment to realize it wasn't real.

Throughout the day, Miss Juanita brought her juice and crackers and helped her sit up to take tiny bites and tiny sips. Sometimes she helped her to the bathroom and then back into bed.

"Whatever you've got, Autumn, it's fierce," she would say as she tucked the covers up under her chin. "You should go back to sleep."

Autumn slept and woke and slept and woke. She wanted to stay asleep, and she wanted to keep dreaming. Whatever was going on in the dream world, it was important.

That evening, Emma came over with her homework and left it with Autumn's mother. Autumn could hear her best friend through the door, asking if they could talk for just a minute. Mama was worried that whatever Autumn had, Emma would catch too, and she promised her that Emma could catch her daughter up on all the gossip next time. Emma left a couple of notes she'd written for Autumn and a picture she drew of Captain McDogs—a half-man, half-dog character she was designing for her comic book. He had a dog's head and a really muscled man's body. Emma was a crazy good artist. In the picture she'd drawn on loose-leaf, the captain had a speech balloon that said it was Autumn's *duty* to get better soon. She smiled weakly at the picture and asked Mama to hang it up on her bulletin board. Then she fell back asleep.

Any time she was awake, Roy was there to tell her a story, but she kept drifting off and missing the middle or the end. Sometimes she would dream the ending. Once when Roy was telling her how they took a trip to Las Vegas for Great-Pop's twenty-first birthday, she dreamed that they both became rich hotel owners and that Great-Pop was going to celebrate his birthday on the top floor of his casino, and she and Roy and Great-Mom were the only ones who were invited.

At one point that evening, Mama drew her a bath and helped her into the tub, sitting on the closed lid of the toilet to keep watch and make sure she didn't slip under the water. Autumn was so sick, she couldn't even feel embarrassed by her mother's presence. One minute she was talking to her mother with her head against the side of the tub, the next she started awake as Mama pulled the stopper in the drain. The water had gone cold. Roy was in the bathroom then too, she noticed, and she demanded he not peek.

Her mother chuckled, misunderstanding. "I grew that body, Autumn. It's nothing I haven't seen before."

"As if I want to look at you, little girl," Roy huffed at the same time, his face turned away from her.

"I don't feel good," she muttered to him.

"I know, princess," he said, less coldly then. "And that worries me. I think it's why you've been coming to the—"

"Come on, sweetheart," Mama said, helping her up onto wobbling legs and wrapping a towel around her. At the moment Autumn's feet touched the fluffy bath mat, the house phone began to ring. The crease between Mama's eyebrows—the one she got when she was particularly worried—came out.

"I've got to get that, baby-doll. That might be work. Can you...? Will you be okay for a minute?"

Autumn nodded, plopping down on the toilet and holding her towel tightly with one hand.

"I'll be right back," she promised, running out of the room before the phone went to voicemail.

"Roy…" Autumn said after a long pause. "I want you to tell me a story."

"All right."

"Not a bad one, though. Not a sad one. I just want a good story. Make one up."

"Make one up? Why would I do that?"

"Make one up about if you hadn't died. If you were still alive, what you would do right now with Great-Pop in the hospital? How you would make him better?" Deciding she wouldn't wait for Mama, she grabbed onto the sink and woozily stood up. "I'm putting my nightgown on now, so keep your head that way." And then she reached for the thin nightgown that hung on the back of the door.

"I told you I won't look."

"Tell me the story." She slipped the cotton material over her head.

"If I was still alive, you wouldn't know your Great-Pop."

"I don't understand."

"He wouldn't have married Virginia, and none of her children would have known him."

"Oh." She hadn't thought about that. "Then tell me another story where we all know each other. And you're alive and things are nice."

Looking in the mirror at her pale face and water-darkened hair, Autumn frowned. Her eyes were glassy and her cheeks blazing red.

"Go to bed," he told her.

"You won't tell me a story?"

"Go to bed," he repeated, "and I'll think about it."

ONCE UPON a time….

AUTUMN BOUND through the front door of The Misters McMillans' house, her hand flying over the wood in a semblance of a knock before she took the key from around her neck and let herself in. They were long past propriety; the two men were more like grandfathers to her than friends of the family. She kicked her muddy shoes off near the doorway. It had been a good day. She felt good about her English test, and Hunter had talked to her after class.

"Hello?" she called into the kitchen. It was raining outside, and she'd run all the way from school through the downpour to the McMillans' home. "Roy? Tommy?" She shivered in the cold air. She was going to need a hot bath. "Are you guys here?"

No answer. Come to think of it, she hadn't seen either of their cars in the driveway.

Rudy and Oscar trotted into the kitchen to greet her, their tails wagging. Rudy whimpered, and Oscar jumped up. That was strange. They always put the dachshunds in their kennels if they weren't going to be home.

Autumn made herself comfortable at their kitchen table. She slung her wet book bag onto the polished wood and reached for the plastic tub of orange jelly slices. They were her favorite candy. One time she'd challenged Tommy to a slice-off, swearing she could eat the whole tub herself in one sitting. But the thick, sugarcoated candy was too much for her, and she gave up after only ten pieces. Tommy smirked at her and told her not to challenge an old man at his own game.

After she had licked the last crystals of sugar off her fingertips, Autumn dug in her bag and pulled out her math book, graph paper, and her pencils. She set to work, plotting lines and figuring equations. Math was her least favorite subject, but she was good at it—thanks to Roy's help. He'd tutored her extensively when she was still in middle school.

"HOW OLD am I in this story?" Autumn whispered with her eyes closed.

"Are you going to listen?"

"I'm older than I am now, though," she argued. "I'm in high school?"

"Yes."

"Why? Why is Great-Pop okay longer in this story? What about you being alive meant he didn't have his stroke when I was twelve, like now?"

"It's a story, Autumn. You wanted a story, I'm telling you one."

"I'm glad."

"Okay."

"I'm glad that he's okay longer. I'm glad you're alive, Roy."

"I'm *not* alive. It's just a story. Keep listening."

IT WAS a quarter to five when she finally finished the last problem. Mrs. Ford was a task master (that was the polite way of putting it), but Autumn never felt it more than with the Monday Night Problems. And there was no skipping over any either, because tomorrow in class she would call on each of them, randomly, and they would be forced to answer a problem. If they made a mistake, she would drag them up in front of the class to work the problem on the chalkboard so the other students could "help" figure out where they'd gone wrong. She'd been called up once for a small calculation error. If the mockery from the other students was "help," she didn't want to be around when they intended to wound.

Autumn checked her problems again, quickly, not really focusing as well as she should, and she shoved all the paperwork back in her bag. The dogs shifted at her feet, whimpering.

"Have you guys been out yet?"

Where were Roy and Tommy? She'd showed up at their house when they were out before, of course—that's why she had the key, to let herself in. But usually they'd just taken a walk around the park or had gone down to the neighbor's house to have coffee and talk. They were always back here by now. Autumn was tapping her eraser against the table, frowning, when the phone rang.

She wasn't sure she should answer it—since it wasn't her house—but she could always say "McMillan residence," and she could ask to take a message. That's what they did on television. She couldn't imagine her friends would mind too much. She jumped up, her chair scraping against the linoleum, and she grabbed the phone on the last ring.

"McMillan residence," she gasped into the receiver.

There was a moment's pause, and then she heard Roy on the other end, a little stiff. "Autumn?"

"Where are you?" she asked playfully. "I've been here for forty-five minutes, waiting for you and Tommy to—"

"Autumn, something bad's happened. Tommy was in an accident. He-he's dead."

"WHAT?" AUTUMN—young, sick Autumn, in her pink covers—demanded as forcefully as she could, which, admittedly, was not very forceful. "What do you mean Tommy's dead?"

"Just what I said," Roy replied plainly.

"I don't like this story *at all*, Roy."

"You asked me to tell you a story about what would have happened if Tommy went into the hospital and I were still alive."

"You made this up."

"Of course I made it up," he said. "You asked me to make up a story."

"You let him die!" she whispered, tears welling in her eyes. "That isn't what I wanted at all."

"Autumn? Tommy can't live forever. When it's his time, it's his time. If he collapsed at the drugstore and I was still alive, maybe I'd have been with him and could have gone with him to the hospital. I would have sat beside him after he was out of the ICU. But it's not as if I can keep a man alive when he's meant to die."

"He's not meant to die!" she cried. "You just don't care enough, Roy McMillan!"

"I would tell him I loved him and that if he needed to go, I'd see him soon."

"You'd *let* him *die*."

"I'd let him *go*."

"I hate you, Roy," she whispered, pulling the covers over her head. "Go away."

"It's just that sometimes, you have to let a person *go*, Autumn."

"Go away, Roy," she repeated, more forcefully this time. "I don't want to talk to you anymore. It's not your decision to let him go or not, and I'm glad you're not here." She stopped herself from saying she was glad he was dead. "I'm glad you're not here if you would just let him go. That means you don't love him enough!" The effort of arguing with Roy made her chest hurt, and she gasped for breath as she pushed through her tears. "But I love him more than enough, and my love is going to keep him alive forever."

"Autumn."

"You can't have him!" she hissed. "I won't let you have him!"

Her sleep was fitful that evening, and she threw up bile more than once. She couldn't believe Roy. He wouldn't have just let Great-Pop go like that! He wouldn't have just let him pass away! He would have fought forever for him. He'd *lied* to her. Roy never would have just said good-bye. And now she understood exactly what he wanted. He wanted her to tell Great-Pop it was okay if he died, so Great-Pop could go be with Roy. But she wouldn't do it, because she loved him the most in the world, and Roy was just being *selfish*.

CHAPTER 22

EVERY EVENING they ate together in the royal dining room with its many large, open windows. That particular evening a cool, rain-scented breeze wafted through the room, and the sound of the rain outside those windows was all the dinnertime accompaniment they needed. Even Reina, when her heart wasn't filled with frustration at being kept from her dear Toren, announced that she thought the kingdom was quite beautiful in its own special way.

They dined on fresh dandelion salad, roasted quail with brioche and chorizo stuffing, and a rich lemon cake, all accompanied by the sweetest white wine. Rook sat at the head of the long table, Toren purposely at the other end, and Princess Reina was forced to sit between them. When she'd made to pull her chair right up next to Toren, Rook asked if she'd prefer to dine alone, and she moved her chair, sullenly, back to the middle of the table. She was more suspicious of Rook than ever, and she kept casting him angry sidelong glances.

Toren, still embarrassed by how that kiss had moved him, was not at all pleased to be under Rook's thumb. Even more than that, he hated seeing Reina becoming more resentful of Rook and less happy every day. There was a part of him that felt it was right for her to be on the throne instead of down on her hands and knees doing manual labor. She looked very elegant in her elaborately embroidered dresses, and when she held court with gold-dust villagers, she really shined. He'd watched, one day, as she addressed the apothecary's concerns in confident and caring tones. Like a true princess.

"We should take a turn through the maze garden, princess," Toren suggested, wanting to draw her attention away from Rook. If her eyes could throw daggers, their captor would be dead twice over. Toren much preferred for her to smile.

Somewhere in the back of his heart, it was there, the sense that if he would submit to what Rook wanted, somehow, having his memories returned to him would change everything. It was only a thought, but perhaps if he remembered what Rook wanted him to remember, then Rook would not be so possessive of him. He would then allow Toren and Reina more time together. The storm clouds in her eyes would fade, and they could all be good companions.

But it was, after all, just a thought. What if he went to bed with Rook and found himself falling further? What if, once Rook had taken Toren, he broke his vow and sent Reina away forever? Denying Rook what he wanted was the only bargaining chip Toren had.

And yet it was getting more difficult and not just because he longed to have his memories back.

There was something about the other man that drew him. Something familiar. And he found he was becoming less inclined to hide from Rook. Sometimes, when Toren was exploring the castle, Rook would just appear behind him, with or without Red-Eye. And in those moments when they were alone, Rook would ask, with a wicked smile, to steal a kiss.

"It's not thievery if you ask," Toren would say, which even to his ears wasn't a no. And then Rook would lean in until only a crack of gray-white light shone between their lips, so he could feel Rook's breath when he spoke, and he would always whisper the same thing before pulling back, leaving Toren's mouth unkissed.

"Someday you'll claim your prize."

And Toren would grow hot about it. What prize? What did that mean? And why did he insist on asking to kiss and then not kissing? That was a frustration in itself! Every time Rook leaned close and didn't kiss him, Toren was left grappling with the knowledge that he *wanted* to be kissed.

The last particularly frustrating unkiss had happened that morning when he took a turn through Rook's vast library. The room itself went up and up and up for stories, with alcoves climbing ever higher. There were hidden stairs and rolling ladders. In the center of the ground floor where Toren explored sat a single reading desk with an oil lamp; the rest of the lower space was lined with shelving. Thousands of books. Hundreds of thousands maybe. More books than any one person could read in a lifetime, he thought. And yet he wanted to pull every one off the shelf and look through it. He wanted to get lost in these books.

Still looking up, Toren had turned a corner and almost bumped right into Rook. He was leaning against a wooden cart that was meant to hold the books that needed to be reshelved. There was a stack there, dusty from disuse.

Rook half smiled at Toren and caught a golden curl, tucking it back behind Toren's ear.

"I was thinking about kissing you."

This again! Toren did not say anything, but waited for Rook to move in close and then not follow through on the wicked temptation.

"What do you think about that?"

"I think that you've got nothing but lust on your mind."

"Is that so? Well, my chaste Toren, what's on your mind?"

"Escaping," he lied. He was thinking about Rook's lips, the way they felt, their warmth, and their pressure. And before that he'd been thinking about exploring the stables behind the palace. Sometimes when he was wandering the southern rooms, he caught a glimpse of them out one of the many windows. He wondered what sort of horses Rook kept. He did not know if he knew how to ride, but he felt confident he could learn. Then he could explore the whole of these lands much more easily.

"You're lying," Rook said, his smile widening. "You think about it less and less every day, actually. I think that you're thinking that you like my lands. And my mouth, perhaps."

"I liked my Sunset Forest," he reminded Rook, avoiding the question of kissing altogether.

"Yes, but my lands have their own appeal too. And I?" He reached out and ran his thumb over Toren's bottom lip. "I also have my own appeal, don't I?"

"You're a rake."

"Maybe."

For a long moment they only stared at each other, Rook content to wait all day. He was as impossible as his bird servant.

"Just kiss me if you want to do it. You did last time."

"Well, that's almost sweet," Rook mocked, "but you know, something about your tone just doesn't make me believe that it's what *you* want."

Frustration roiling in his heart, Toren leaned forward and placed his lips against Rook's. There was a moment in that rather unromantic kiss when Toren felt something stir—like a memory and an emotion rolled into one. He stumbled forward, shoving the cart out of the way, and grabbed Rook's shoulder. He didn't want to lose this... this flicker of memory! Toren tilted his head and kissed again, his lips searching and willing. And that was when Rook kissed him back. They fell into one of the shelves. It rocked under their combined weight, but did not fall. Neither would have cared if it had. Broken book spines were of no concern in that moment.

Yes, yes! He almost *knew* this. He almost *knew* Rook's mouth—and not from that sensual exchange in the grand hall. He continued to kiss him deeper, felt his tongue, felt that memory flickering, stirring, surging toward the surface. He shoved his hands into Rook's hair and pulled him even closer, pressed against him. So close! Toren was so close to remembering! And then, as quickly as it had happened, their lips broke apart.

"No!" Toren gasped. None of it made sense—the images that the kiss stoked? Where was that place? Who were those people? He blinked hard as Rook put space between them. He'd seen her too, in that flash. Reina smiling, laughing, her red hair flying as he pushed her on the swing. Reina....

"Well then." If Rook had shown him even a moment's kindness then or run a tender finger down his cheek, Toren would have willingly—eagerly—gone to his bed. Not for the return of his memories, but because Rook was right. They *had* known each other. But Rook chose that moment to be distant and arrogant, and he was cool as he said, "I knew there was passion in you, Toren. It's only a matter of time before you submit."

"Go to hell."

"What makes you think I'm not already there?" Rook asked, while grinning.

PRINCESS REINA had been staring at him for a good long while; he was suddenly aware of this. Toren was aware too, that hot color flushed up one side of his face. His memories were giving him away.

"I'm sorry, princess. Did you say something?"

"I said that I would love to go with you to the garden maze." Then, tossing an annoyed glance at Rook, she added, "But *he* says that I have elocution lessons, and then I'm supposed to practice my harp, and then it's an early bedtime. I'm holding court in the morning."

It was not lost on Toren that Reina had stopped speaking Rook's name—instead calling him "he" or "him" or "the bastard" during those stolen moments when they were alone together or when he managed to gain an audience with her by waiting in a line of gold-dust villagers.

"Surely she has time to walk through the maze?" Toren asked. Rook met his eyes with a firm blue gaze and did not balk.

"If she would take her lessons more seriously during the day." Rook shrugged.

"If only my lessons had *meaning*," she complained, slamming her small palms down on the table. Her sleeves covered her hands to the fingertips. "You know that they were designed to keep me away from Toren. The people I'm meeting aren't even *real*. They're just figments!"

"Look at you, princess," Rook replied calmly, "disrupting a meal with your childish anger? You are sorely in need of your lessons."

She glared at him, her flat chest rising and falling in anger. "I can go home whenever I want to, and when I do, I will do everything in my power to wake him up. And then what will happen, *Rook*? He'll leave this place, won't he?"

Rook's bemused grin faded, and he sized up the young girl, now his full-fledged opponent. "He won't resist me for much longer."

"If he's not here anymore, there won't be anything to resist."

"And if you leave this place to go wake him—assuming you could *wake him*—then you leave him open and vulnerable to me."

"Would someone please tell me just what it is that you're talking about?" Toren demanded. They were arguing in cryptic code, and he was certain he was the subject. He pushed his plate away and sat back in his chair.

"He wants to take you from me," Princess Reina told Toren sourly.

"And she doesn't know when it's time to *let go*," Rook replied.

"I don't understand what either of you is on about. And why you can't just get along. And...."

"Share?" Rook finished quietly. "There is no sharing. She's not meant for this place."

"And neither is he!" she exclaimed hotly, pointing straight at Toren's face. "And I will do everything I can to bring him back to me!"

CHAPTER 23

THEY BROUGHT Great-Pop home from the hospital on Wednesday. Mama came in with some medicine and the news. Autumn smiled brightly, and when she struggled to sit up, Mama pushed her back against the mattress.

"C'mon, baby-doll, you're still not feeling well. Please don't try to get up."

"I need to go see Great-Pop. Is he awake? Is he talking? Did he ask for me?"

Mama looked sad for a moment, and she shook her head. "He hasn't woken up, but there's nothing more they can do at the hospital right now. He's going home, and Aunt Amy Jo is going to stay with him and Great-Mom during the day."

Autumn frowned. She didn't like this *at all*. What sort of hospital turned a person out when they were still sick? And wasn't a coma practically the most sick you could be? She asked Mama as much, and her mother sighed.

"Oh baby-doll, you've got no idea. The damned insurance company won't pay for another night." She inhaled and exhaled, once, twice, and then put her annoyingly optimistic face on. "But it's okay. It's going to be okay." She pushed long strands of red hair out of Autumn's face. "And hey, we can go visit him when you're feeling better."

"I feel great," she out and out lied. "Let's go now."

"Let me rephrase. We'll go when you aren't sleeping eighteen hours a day, when you can keep your food down, and when your temperature is back to normal."

"Mama," she started to beg as her mother walked toward the bedroom door, but changed directions at her mother's "don't argue" look. "Can I ask you something?"

Her mother nodded.

"Where do you think we go when we die?"

The question obviously startled her, because Mama stiffened just a little, like she did when people asked her to join them at church. And then, looking at her daughter's face, she sighed and said, "Honestly, baby-doll, I really just don't know. I like to think we go somewhere happy and warm."

"Yeah? Do you think we go to heaven?"

"Maybe. I don't know that I really believe in heaven and hell like they're written in the Bible, but maybe something like that. Some place where we can all meet again and be happy together and healthy."

"Like a forest where the sun never sets," she whispered, and her mother smiled encouragingly, nodding her head.

"Maybe." She walked back over and sat down on the edge of Autumn's bed. The mattress gave just a little under her weight. "I think my 'heaven,' if you want to call it that, will be a room full from floor to ceiling with pillows where I can sleep all the time."

Autumn grinned and closed her eyes. "Can I come there?"

"It wouldn't be heaven without you," she replied firmly. "And I'd be pretty put out—when I wasn't sleeping and enjoying the peace and quiet—if you didn't at least come visit me from time to time."

"Mama?" she asked again. "What if Great-Pop doesn't…? What if, Great-Pop dies, and he doesn't want me in his heaven?"

Her mother reached out and caught Autumn's hand. Autumn's eyes opened. "Why are you so worried about this all of a sudden? Did someone say something to you at that church?"

"No. I just…." She couldn't tell Mama that Roy wanted Great-Pop with him and that he had no room in his heart for her. What happened when Great-Pop finally did go to that place? Would he have no room in his heart for her either? He'd been with Roy first. Autumn didn't come along until much, much later. Roy had died and lost his claim, but if Great-Pop died too, couldn't Roy stake claim on his heart all over again?

"Listen to me, Autumn. Your Great-Pop loves you so much. From the moment you were born and we put you in his arms, he was in love with you. And nothing in this world or out of it is going to change that." Her voice caught, and she tried to fight off tears by feebly waving her hand in the air. "I'm *sure* he's going to be fine. Maybe a little *different* when he wakes up. Strokes do sad things to people. But even if he is different, Autumn, he will always love you."

"I just don't want him to forget me if he…."

"You have a special place in his heart. No one and nothing can take it away."

When she was alone in the room, Autumn turned toward her window. She hoped her mother was right, but she couldn't be certain. Roy was jealous and mean and selfish, and she thought he really didn't want Great-Pop to love her anymore. He had a lot of power in her reality and in his. Especially in his.

She lay back against her pillow and thought. She had to get better as quickly as possible, and when she wasn't awake, she had to go back to the valley and defend "Toren." It had taken her a while to realize she was having the dreams about the same place every night and even longer still to understand she was dreaming with a strange sort of continuity. When she awoke the night before, her clock glowing 2:48 a.m., she remembered *everything*. They weren't distorted pieces of dream-fluff, but real, solid memories. She remembered the Sunset Cottage and the Rain Kingdom and Toren and Rook and Red-Eye, and she remembered herself as the defiant Princess Reina.

BOTH MAMA and Miss Juanita expressed their surprise the next day when she ate a full bowl of cereal for breakfast—and kept it down! She focused on her breathing, on keeping her heart calm as she thoroughly chewed each bite. She was eating for Great-Pop. She took her medicine when she was asked, and she rested, even though she was starting to get antsy just lying around all day. Miss Juanita let her move to the couch and watch her stories with her. Mama didn't like soap operas—said they were all trashy—but Autumn thought they were great. She especially liked when Miss Juanita explained all about the story they weren't showing on the screen. She was a pretty good storyteller.

"That's the second Dirk Turner; the first one died in the eighties. So it's sort of a joke on the show that he doesn't really age. Because the second actor was about half his age when he took over the role. But we didn't really care—he's a good-looking fella."

He was sort of handsome, Autumn thought, for an older man. Definitely no Joey Sullivan. Juanita knew a lot about the actors on her stories, and she remembered years and years of backstory.

"A lot of people have forgotten that Crystal had an affair with Rock and that she got pregnant and gave up the baby, but I haven't forgiven her. What she did to Bryce, I've been mad about it for ten years."

When Mama paid Miss Juanita for the day and she went home, Autumn asked if she could try sitting at the table for dinner. Mama thought about it and nodded. "All right, but if you start to get woozy—"

"I'll go right to bed," Autumn lied. She'd have to slump right out of her chair before she admitted she was feeling woozy at all. She *had* to prove to Mama she was getting better. And this was how the rest of her week went, with her showing by small degrees that she was feeling better—by eating her meals, by doing her homework, by obeying all of Mama's rules, even when she felt so antsy she couldn't stand it. Finally, on Saturday, she was able to see Emma, who brought her seven more notes, a story about Miss Proctor's skirt splitting when she bent over, and news about Hunter. "He asked about you!" Emma exclaimed with a smile. "He wants to know if you're feeling better."

"Really?" she asked. She hadn't thought about Hunter all week, but that was really nice. Actually, it was really, *really* nice.

"He wrote you this note." Emma dug it out from her pocket. "And yes, I did read it, but I knew you wouldn't mind."

"You didn't show it to anyone else, right?"

"No." Emma shook her head solemnly. "And Ronni was asking about it, but I swear I didn't tell her anything. She's such a loudmouth."

Despite having already read the note, Emma sat beside Autumn and pored over every word with her. It was only a few lines, but the girls analyzed everything from the "Dear Autumn" to the lack of "love, Hunter" to his sloppy handwriting.

Dear Autumn,
I know you aren't feeling well. I hope you get better soon.
—Hunter

"He has to write it like that," Emma insisted, as if she thought Autumn would be heartbroken that the boy wasn't more showy. "He can't be all like 'I think you're beautiful and I miss your face every single day.' What if someone read the letter instead of you?"

"Like you?" Autumn laughed.

She was so glad to see Emma again—she'd been going into best friend withdrawals, even though they'd been talking on the phone for the last few nights. It wasn't the same as getting to actually hang out together. The fact that Mama let Emma in must mean she thought Autumn was getting well. They talked for a long time until Emma finally said she had to get home unless she wanted to get grounded into the next decade. Then she asked if Autumn wanted to sleep over the next weekend if she was feeling well, and Autumn enthusiastically said yes.

After Emma left, Autumn took a shower and got dressed—really all the way dressed, in jeans and a Vanity concert T-shirt—for the first time all week. She hesitantly went to the living room. Mama was on the phone with her "friend" Jack again. They were being mushy. Autumn tried not to eavesdrop… too much. She casually kicked the back of the couch to let Mama know she was there. From the way her mother jumped, it was obvious she hadn't been expecting her out of bed.

After she hurriedly (and way too obviously) ended the call, Autumn said, "Mama, do you think we can go visit Great-Pop now?"

For a long time, her mother just sat there, like she was getting ready to say no. Autumn knew from experience that if she pestered, the answer would automatically *be* no, so she kept her mouth shut, even biting down on her lip. The urge to ask if her mother was still thinking about it was almost overwhelming.

Finally, after forever, Mama said, "All right, but it will need to be a short visit."

"And I can sit with him? And talk to him?" she asked, because of course the last time she'd been so close to him, Aunt Vivian and Uncle Jacob and Uncle Greg had screwed the whole thing up.

"Of course."

Great-Mom greeted them at the door when they arrived. She hugged Mama lightly and then Autumn let herself be hugged. She didn't really like Great-Mom's hugs. They were so delicate, just like the tiny china teacups she brought out and wouldn't let any of the children touch. It was like she thought a real hug, the kind Autumn loved where you wrapped your arms around a person and near smothered them, would break her. Mama said Great-Mom had osteoporosis and her bones were fragile, but Autumn wondered if maybe that was just an excuse. She thought Great-Mom just didn't want to give real hugs. Because who ever heard of a hug breaking a bone?

"Thank you for coming," Great-Mom said with her politest smile, and Autumn nodded because it was expected of her. She couldn't think of a single thing to say to Great-Mom. For a minute she thought about Virginia sipping her lemonade with Tommy, accepting his marriage proposal with quiet happiness. She probably gave the same horrible hugs back then too.

"Can I see Great-Pop?" Autumn asked impatiently.

Apparently her mother thought she was being rude, because she clucked. "Autumn. Let's visit with Great-Mom for a while."

But Great-Mom didn't mind that Autumn hadn't come to visit with her. She said genially, "Of course, dear. He's in the guest bedroom."

Autumn hurried past her, through the kitchen, down the hall, and to the farthest bedroom. Any other time she might have been annoyed that they didn't have Great-Pop in his own bed. Today, she didn't care. She burst through the door, ready to face down any aunt, uncle, cousin, grandparent, or family friend who thought to deny her what she'd been waiting for. Instead she found Great-Pop alone, slightly inclined against the lavender pillows, the window open to reveal a brilliantly beautiful sunset. He looked like he was sleeping. The sight of him startled her, and she stopped for a moment.

"Great-Pop?" she whispered. And then "Tommy?" And "Toren?"

She resisted the urge to shake him, reminding herself that it couldn't do any good. She quietly shut the bedroom door and sat in the small armchair nearby. When she was a little girl, Great-Pop showed her a place in the closet where the floorboards could come up.

"What is it?" she'd asked.

"Trapdoor," he said. "It goes under the house."

She'd never been brave enough to go down there before. Now, she'd have crawled under there in the dark, faced any scorpion or spider, if he would just open his eyes.

"Hi, Great-Pop," she said, a little louder than she normally would. She wasn't sure how loud she had to talk if she wanted to be heard. "I've been waiting to see you for so long. I'm sorry I couldn't come sooner. It's Autumn, if you can't tell by my voice."

She thought for a moment. There were dozens of stories about his time with Roy rattling around in her head. And if Roy hadn't been so mean to her and made it so clear he wanted to take Great-Pop from her, she would have tried telling him one. Instead, she thought about their last family reunion. She was ten and a half, and Mama made fried chicken, and Aunt Fifi's husband, Denny, got drunk and fell into the river.

CHAPTER 24

AUTUMN LAY out on the large blue-and-white checkered blanket, staring up at the sky. It was a brilliantly blue day, with fluffy white clouds that went on as far as the eye could see. Her stomach was full to bursting with fried chicken and mashed potatoes and two helpings of corn on the cob and Aunt Carma's chocolate crumble pie. Some of the other, older, kids were down by the river playing with the old tire swing. Hannah said, grudgingly, that Autumn could come along if she wasn't going to be a *tattletale* and a *nerd*, but Autumn told her no. She liked some of her other cousins and even the aunts and uncles she had that were only a few years older than she was. She just couldn't stand Hannah.

The reunion was the largest she'd ever been to, with almost every single family member flying or driving in to attend. They brought with them their large families and their friends and their boyfriends and even some ex-spouses who were still on good terms with everyone. And there were so many of them they'd had to reserve three full plots at the lake, and even then it was a little crowded.

Everyone brought so much food. There were so many delicious things to eat that even though she only got a little bit of everything she wanted, she was way too stuffed. It was a good day, and her stomach was being kind to her. Mama seemed to know just about everyone, or she faked it really well, because she moved from group to group and hugged people and chatted while Autumn hung back and listened. She didn't like strangers, but when Mama forced her forward, she smiled as well as she could manage and talked about school and her favorite classes. If they still wanted to know more about her, she talked about Emma. At the first opportunity, though, she grabbed her plate of food and ran for the blanket.

Things were winding down just a little then. Those who had only come to put in a brief appearance had packed up their minivans with leftovers and children—presumably their own—and headed out. A lot of the adults had gone down to the river to float or fish or drink on the shore. And the rest were milling about, quieter now that their bellies were full. Daddy, who'd come at the last minute after complaining about it all morning, was passed out under a tree. A food coma, Emma would say. Autumn could hear some of her aunts talking about one her uncle's new girlfriend from their matching lawn chairs, and on the other side, a ways down near the barbecue pit, her cousin told a friend of hers how their grandma used to be a beauty queen.

Autumn let out a long, contented sigh and traced the outer edges of the largest cloud with her eyes. She'd just about decided it was a monkey peeling a banana when Great-Pop came hobbling up the hill holding two popsicles. She smiled at him and waved without sitting up. She was way too full for a popsicle, but she didn't tell him that. She just scooched over and let him have his place on the blanket. He moved slowly, his knees creaking as he sank to the ground, and she had to be really patient as she waited.

"What do you think of the reunion?" he asked.

"It's big this year."

"Yeah," he agreed with a smile. "I'm thinking people don't reckon Great-Mom and I will make it to the next one, so they thought to come out now."

Autumn laughed because she misunderstood what he meant. "You going to skip the next one?"

"Maybe," he agreed with a wink. "So what are you doing over here all by your pretty lonesome? Why aren't you down playing with the other kids?"

"I don't know," she lied. She didn't want to tell him she didn't like Hannah very much, in case he did. "I'm just cloud watching. I'm guessing the shapes." She smiled. "There's a monkey." But the wind had pushed it farther along that expanse of blue sky. It looked more like a bride with a trailing veil now. She shrugged. "What are you doing?"

"Bringing a popsicle to my favorite girl."

This made her giggle, and she nibbled on the end of the freezing treat. Hers was green and so cold it hurt her teeth. He had one too, a purple one, but he couldn't manage more than a few licks before he was complaining about his dentures. She asked him if he wanted her to eat it for him, which was how she ended up with two popsicles too many.

"Great-Pop?" she asked. "Do you ever look at shapes in the clouds?"

"Not as much as I should," he said. "I used to do it a lot, when my chores were done. We had this great spot on the bank, and I'd lay there and watch the clouds. But that's been, I don't know, your age times eight?"

"You should try it," she insisted and let her body fall back against the hard ground. She studied the sky, trying to find another good one. In the far distance, she could just make out one that looked like a willow tree moving gently in the breeze.

Down near the river, Uncle Denny was dancing on the end of the pier, a beer in each hand. It was obvious that, like her popsicles, he had two beers too many, because he ended up tripping over his own feet and falling, dramatically, face-first into the muddy water. Aunt Fif's laughter carried all the way up the bank to where they were sitting.

"I don't think I'm going to drink when I get older," she said. Daddy drank but he never danced on the pier. He just got sour and shut down. Either way, she was pretty sure beer made people stupid.

"Probably wise," Great-Pop agreed. "Can't think of anything good that ever came of it. Except...." His smile was a private one, and she nudged him when he didn't continue.

"Are you thinking of a Roy story?" she asked, a touch excitedly. It had been a while since he told her one, and she was ready. She propped herself up on her elbows.

"Yes, but it's a little too PG-13 for you, kiddo."

She frowned. He'd never denied her a Roy story before. She tried to think of a work-around. She asked him to leave out the bad parts, and he laughed and told her it was almost entirely made of bad parts.

There was a long pause, and then he said, "Sometimes I don't think I'm fair to Virginia." Autumn really didn't know what to make of that. She looked over to where Great-Mom was standing at the drinks table. She very carefully dipped the ice scoop into the bucket and filled plastic cups full of ice. She looked up at the pair of them, as if she'd heard her name. And she waved and smiled, and Great-Pop waved back. "I should tell you a story about Virginia and me."

"But I want to hear about Roy," she argued, a touch insulted by the prospect of another story altogether.

"I understand that, princess, but I worry that you don't really know about your Great-Mom the way that maybe you should. I worry you don't know how good she's been. I should tell you a story about her."

"She's been good," Autumn agreed. She didn't want to hear any stories about Great-Mom, who was so stiff and polite and breakable and *old*. She wanted to hear about Roy. Those stories were always romantic and fun or funny. She looked at him. If it was a choice between a story about Great-Mom and no story at all, *well*, Autumn sulked, *I'd rather have nothing at all.*

"I'm going to go play with Hannah and the others down at the tire swing," she told him, though really she was just going to find somewhere else to sit.

"All right," he agreed, as if he thought nothing of it. He patted her back gently as she stood up and hurried off to find a new spot to watch the clouds. Alone.

"I SHOULD have let you tell me your story," Autumn whispered in the still room. She took his large, limp hand in both of hers and squeezed tight enough that she hoped he could feel her. "But you can tell me now, Great-Pop. I'm listening. We don't ever have to talk about Roy again. You've got fifty years of stories about Great-Mom, and I want to hear them all. So please just wake up and tell me."

He didn't, of course. He continued to lie there, his body unmoving as if he were sleeping. Autumn closed her eyes and sighed. She wouldn't give up on him, not for anything in the world. She'd come back tomorrow, and the next day, and the day after, and every day until he woke up. And she would continue to tell him her stories, the stories he had given to her first.

That night she went to bed early, and not just because she had school in the morning. Mama tucked her in, like she had when Autumn was still a little girl, and kissed her forehead, which was finally cool after so many days of running a fever.

"How was it for you? Visiting with Great-Pop?"

"Fine," Autumn fibbed. She had really, truly believed he would wake up if she could just talk to him. She didn't understand how he could sleep through the sound of her voice and her pleas that he come back to her. But she was determined not to give up. Every night since she'd gotten sick, she had ended up back where Roy was posing as Rook and Great-Pop thought his name was Toren. She would go there tonight, and she would take his hand, and she would tell him that she was waiting for him back *home*. She would do her best to hold on to him even when she woke up, and somehow drag him out of that place.

CHAPTER 25

REINA BLINKED and looked around the elegant throne room with its gilded wallpaper and dangling chandeliers. There was a freshly painted portrait of her and her hounds hanging nearby. She could see it without having to turn her head.

She must have drifted off for just a moment, because everything seemed so fresh and new, including the hundreds of roses meticulously placed around her. The plush, down-filled seat of the throne was delightful, but the numbness in her backside was an uncomfortable reminder that perhaps she'd been sitting a little too long.

When Red-Eye came to announce another dignitary she was to hold court with, Reina raised her delicate hand, heavy today with diamonds and strings of pearls and sapphires, and she smiled. "Please ask the duke to wait just a little longer for me." She liked Red-Eye tremendously, as a bird or as a woman. Even so, Red-Eye could be focused and demanding—obsessed even—as if she wanted nothing more in the world than to serve Rook and cater to his wishes. She was always on his schedule and never expressed any desire except those he'd dictated to her.

Reina got off her throne, stretching in the stiff material of her gown. It was a lovely day, she thought. The rain had let up, just a little. It was only drizzling and the sky was more white than gray. She went to the window nearest the throne and opened it, so she could smell the fresh scents outside. The breeze played with the tendrils of hair at her temples.

Red-Eye followed her to the window, her feathered black hair bouncing behind her as she moved. Reina turned and looked at the crow woman.

"If I could fly like you, Red-Eye, I would travel the whole of these lands and see everything there was to see." In a moment, perhaps because she'd mentioned flying with such reverence, her companion—or more accurately, her watcher—had transformed back into a crow. She hopped along the windowsill. Reina reached out one finger to pet her lovely black feathers. Red-Eye cocked her head suspiciously and then, with obvious reservation, she allowed the princess to touch her for the briefest moment. "Why haven't you delivered my message to the duke?"

"My master wants you to meet with the duke," Red-Eye told her through her open beak. "You should not delay."

"Rook does dote, doesn't he?" she asked, not at all concerned to be monitored. As a princess, she had many important duties, and it was only natural that Rook, who led these lands, would have high expectations of her. "Well, if you want, you can tell him that I am managing my royal duties, but I'm calling for a brief reprieve as my backside has gone numb."

The bird cocked its stately head at her. She giggled.

"I thought to take a turn around the throne room or maybe stretch my legs in the library."

"Please continue to hold court," Red-Eye insisted. "My master wishes that you would."

"All right," she conceded with a dainty sigh, "but at least let me stand for a moment longer."

Red-Eye had hopped down off the window and turned, fluidly, back into a woman, shedding feathers on the carpet like fallen rose petals. Reina quietly closed the windows. She would not explore or wander now. Instead, she took only a moment to glide back and forth across the room in her long, ivy-green dress before reseating herself on the throne. The whole time Red-Eye stood sentry, watching her.

"I'm ready to meet with the duke," she finally said, lifting her jeweled scepter off a velvet pillow nearby. She held it aloft as she'd been taught and waited as Rook's servant glided down the steps to retrieve her next petitioner.

He was ghostly and insubstantial, trailing golden dust flakes in his wake until she smiled at him. Her smile gave him form, and when he saw her, he bowed. A portly man with a reddened face and a big, boisterous laugh, the duke was one of her favorite gold-dust citizens. He came, always, with one purpose. To play chess with the princess—so play they did. He wasn't real, though. None of the royals or aristocrats or peasants who came to her court—who were, supposedly, the peoples of this land—were "real" in the sense that Rook and Toren and she were real. Nor were they like Rook's servant, Red-Eye, who was really just a crow. The men and women and sometimes children who Reina listened to day after day were, rather, ideas, placeholders, filler in the Rain Kingdom. They brought her conflict and requests and stories and presents, and she did her best to listen to them with her whole heart. Even if they weren't real, for the moment at least, they were speaking with her. They depended on her for guidance. She enjoyed meeting with them. She enjoyed the challenges they put before her. Her work in the throne room was valid. After all, there might come a day when these lands would be populated by others like she and Rook and Toren.

After she had met with her last supplicant—the keeper of the orphanage who asked for a stipend to place children in good homes—Reina went to the music room and played the solitary piano which sat far from the door. There were lamps she could light, but enough daylight filtered in through the high windows that it was unnecessary. She played for a long time, the same notes over and over again, until she felt she'd mastered the piece, and then she practiced her singing in the empty theater. Finally, when it grew late, she retired to her room to embroider while Red-Eye brushed out her long, red hair and braided it back, over and over again. Reina liked it here. She liked the peace of the days, and she liked being a princess.

"My master wishes that you would come to dinner," Red-Eye told her. Red-Eye always knew what Rook wanted. They didn't even have to be in the same room. Indeed, the bird woman had not left Reina's side all day, but she knew the hour, and she knew her master's wishes.

Reina nodded and allowed her hair to be twisted up into a bun and pinned into a net with gems and flowers. Then she set her embroidery aside and followed Red-Eye to the dining hall.

With a gracious curtsy to the room at large, Reina took her place at the middle of the table. One of the gold-dust servants brought them a meal of lamb and baby potatoes with rose herbs and the most delicious chocolate mousse she had ever tasted. Reina moaned after every bite and couldn't hide her sunny smile for anything. The meal was too delicious, and she complimented the table at large, delighted by her whole day. Toren looked very pleased with her, for reasons she didn't understand, and Rook surveyed her—as always—a touch coolly. Well, with food like this in her belly, how could she be upset with his distance? She raised her glass of sparkling cider at him and smiled.

"Thank you for a lovely day, Master Rook."

He continued to stare at her for a moment before he nodded. "No complaints, then, I trust?"

"None." She giggled. "Though, I would like to make certain that I practice my dressage tomorrow." She thought of the mares in the stables with their gentle eyes and their sleek manes and tails. They were restless to get out and play in the rain, but she'd spent far too long at the piano today. "There simply aren't enough hours in the day for all the things I would like to do."

"What about your precious Toren?" Rook asked slowly, gauging her response. His eyes flicked over to the end of the table.

She looked at Toren as well and smiled apologetically. "Well, yes, of course I'd like to see you too, Toren. It's just that there's so much I must attend to! You should request an audience with me tomorrow—if you have the time."

"You're really coming into your own, princess," Toren said, and though he was smiling, he seemed a touch sad.

"I guess I am," she agreed enthusiastically, and pierced a baby potato with her silver fork. "I can't believe I was scrubbing floors when I came to this place."

"Toren?" Rook asked with a long, steady look, "Our Princess Reina seems to understand her role a bit better today. Might you, also, be ready to—?"

Toren's look darkened. "I've no need for your *prize*."

"You don't want your memories back?" Reina asked quietly. She herself was quite content without hers—not remembering a thing before her time in the Sunset Forest. Except, there was still the lure of home. As enchanting as the Rain Kingdom was, she knew she had to return there.

That evening, as she dressed down for bed, Reina realized that her day really had been close to perfect. She lay down on the large, cool, mattress and let Red-Eye tuck the covers up under her chin.

"My master says you should go home now, princess."

She felt drowsy, floating on waves of satisfaction. "Yes…," she said., "Yes, I think I should."

"My master hopes you've enjoyed your time in his kingdom. He feels, though, that you should not return."

"But what of Toren?" she asked. "Doesn't he need me?"

"Master will take care of him."

And with an unpracticed hand, Red-Eye gently patted her on the shoulder.

"You needn't worry."

"I needn't," Reina agreed, and then she was asleep.

CHAPTER 26

"No." Autumn's breath stabbed the still darkness as her eyes flew open. She'd been *right there*! She could remember every moment of the dream! She'd felt the droplets of rain on her skin when she'd held her hands out the window that evening to gather water to rinse her face. She'd heard the lovely sounds of harp music coming from the salon where an imaginary citizen played. She could still taste lamb on her tongue! But she'd been completely oblivious while she was there. She'd been a *moron*! Devoid of anything that made her Autumn. She couldn't control her limbs but watched herself moving from the outside as she played the dutiful part of Rook's pawn. Even if she'd had control and could have gone where she pleased and said what she wanted, there was no thought in her head of Great-Pop and Roy or anything beyond the Rain Kingdom. What had happened? Why didn't she have control and cognizance there anymore?

She stared, bleary-eyed, at the clock on her nightstand. It wasn't even 5:00 a.m., but try as she might, she couldn't go back to sleep.

School that morning was awkward despite the fact that she had the coolest friends in the world. They'd all decorated her locker with notes and pictures and glitter and a bouquet of Joey Sullivan photographs. She smiled as she broke through the crepe paper that had "locked" her door in place, but despite the surprise, she couldn't shake the feeling she was out of step with the rest of the school. Even though she'd done all the homework Emma had brought her, she still felt like the other kids knew things she didn't. And lots of people seemed to be talking about her or whispering whenever they saw her.

"They aren't!" Emma promised kindly, between classes. She'd thrown an arm around Autumn's shoulders. "Believe me, I know because I felt exactly like that when I had my surgery."

"But the last thing that happened was I was called to the office, and then I was gone for a bunch of days. I mean, that's going to make people think weird stuff."

"Yeah, but I told 'em that your great gramps was in the hospital, and then you got sick. Not with the same thing. They were bored with it before I even finished talking. Don't worry. I'll beat up anyone who gives you crap."

Then she passed Autumn another note, ("In case you get bored in class," Emma had said) expertly folded with a little pull tab. She'd drawn flowers all over the front and back. It was probably about a new boy she liked. Autumn stuffed the note into her book bag.

In math class, Hunter asked how she was feeling, and she told him she was a lot better. He stared for a really long minute, like he expected her to say something else. When she didn't, he blushed and turned back to the front of the class. She felt bad for not knowing what else to say. Maybe thank you, at least, for the note he'd sent home with Emma. For thinking about her. She studied the back of his neck where his hair didn't quite meet his collar. If she reached out and poked him, she could still say thank you. It wasn't too late.

The day passed slowly, with only one really embarrassing moment in Social Studies when Mr. Decker called on her to answer a question, and her brain went completely blank. He smiled at her kindly and said something about forgetting that she'd been sick. But she'd done all the homework! It wasn't because she'd been sick. She was just tired, and she couldn't stop thinking about her lack of control when she was in the valley. Autumn didn't know how she was going to do it, but she had to go back to the Rain Kingdom, and she had to *remember* herself when she did.

Autumn gathered up her binder and books and pens for the day and was walking through the school toward the bus loop when Hunter was suddenly walking right beside her. She glanced over at him and blushed.

"Hi," she managed. "Um, thank you for the note. And thank you for asking about me today."

"'Course." He held the door open as she stepped out of the hallway with the flickering light into the bright midafternoon. "Uh… so…."

"What bus are you on?" she asked. All the buses were lined up, their doors open, and kids pushing and shoving each other to get on and get the best seats.

"Oh, I don't ride the bus," he said. "I live, like, five minutes from here, so I just walk home."

Autumn smiled again. There was no reason at all for him to have come out to the bus loop. He'd just followed her.

"I'm on seventy-four," she said, just to have something to say. "You can wait with me for a little while if you want."

Emma was already on the bus. Autumn could see her in their seat near the back, her nose pressed against the window. When she saw that Autumn was walking with Hunter, she made exaggerated eyebrows at her.

"Hey, Autumn?"

"Mm-hmm?" she asked.

"You...." His voice dropped really low. "You remember when we, y'know, kissed on the blacktop?"

She kept her eyes firmly on Emma's face. Emma was pressing her lips against the window and puffing her cheeks out like a blowfish. Autumn was worried everyone around them could hear him, even though she barely could, and they were all too busy goofing off to care anyway.

She nodded one short, tight nod.

"You remember how I told Emma to tell you the guys dared me to do it?"

She nodded again.

"I... uh... sorta lied."

Emma had just started making a pig nose at her when Autumn whipped her head around to face Hunter, eyes wide. "You what?"

"Well, I sort of just wanted to... kiss you. And if I didn't make up an excuse, maybe you, y'know, wouldn't want to kiss me."

The line had moved forward, so she and Hunter were left on the sidewalk with a gap forming between them and the other kids.

"So the guys don't know we kissed then?"

"No one knows."

"Emma knows," Autumn said.

"Well," he said uncertainly. "No one else knows. Unless you told?"

"No, only Emma. And she capital S Swore that she wouldn't tell a soul. She's my best friend. She won't tell."

"Are you mad at me?"

"That it was your idea and not really a dare the guys made up?" Autumn said, and for the first time all day she laughed. Laughed right out loud. She hadn't forgotten what she needed to do when she got home or how serious it all was, but for one second she was able to put it on hold. Hunter helped her put it on hold. "I'm not mad."

"Good."

"You gettin' on, Autumn?" the bus driver asked. An eighth grade girl tore down the sidewalk and leaped onto the bus in front of her. "We're all waiting for you."

"I've gotta go," Autumn said, hitching her backpack higher on her shoulder.

"Okay, I'll see you in class."

"See you."

When she sat down in the seat Emma had saved for her with her large teal backpack, her best friend pulled a piece of loose leaf out of her binder and began to write in exaggerated cursive letters:

So is it L-O-V-E? Y or N? Circle 1

AUTUMN WALKED briskly home from the bus, and the first thing she did after she checked the mailbox was call Mama at work. She called every day after school, just to let her know she'd made it home safe and no weird people had grabbed her off the street. But today, she had a request. She asked, knowing full well what the answer would be, if she could ride her bike over to Great-Pop's. This wouldn't work, because her great-grandparents lived across the highway. She tried anyway.

"I don't think so," Mama said slowly, as if this was the first time her headstrong daughter had ever broached the subject.

"I really want to go see him," Autumn explained, trying to keep the whine out of her voice. Mama hated whining. "I have more stories to tell him. It's really important."

Her mother sighed into the phone. Autumn could hear papers rustling in the background. She knew she wasn't supposed to keep her mother on the line when she was at work.

"Maybe can you take me when you get home?" she asked quickly.

"Actually...." Her mother sighed again, but this sigh had a different quality to it. She sounded almost embarrassed. "Um, actually, tonight, baby-doll, we're having a dinner guest. I'm sorry, I meant to tell you this morning, and it completely slipped my mind."

"Is it Jack?" Autumn asked impatiently.

"You... know about Jack?" Her mother's voice had dropped to a whisper. "Why didn't you say anything? Why—? No, I'm sorry. I'm the one who's been keeping secrets." She cleared her throat and brought her voice back to a reasonable level. "Yes, I thought it would be really nice if I introduced you to Jack. He's been interested in meeting you for a long time. I've told him a lot about you."

"All right," Autumn agreed. She didn't care either way about Mama's new probably-boyfriend. Emma would have been annoyed if her own mother had kept secrets, but it was all Autumn had ever known. Mama tried to protect her—though she was generally bad at it and Autumn always found out long before Mama was ready to reveal the truth. "But what about Great-Pop?"

"Well, I've got to get dinner going when I get home. I guess I could call Aunt Erin and see if she can take you over there, and then maybe I can swing by their house on the way home. That shouldn't make me too late."

"Really?" Autumn asked excitedly.

"Yes, but you need to do your homework after you finish your visit."

"All right!" she agreed, her brain buzzing with plans. "Yes, yes, I will!"

"And Autumn?" her mother continued. "It would be really nice if you would *talk* with Great-Mom. Just for a little while."

She didn't know how to reply to that. She didn't want to talk to Great-Mom. Great-Mom never had anything to say, not to her, anyway. She sniffed and finally agreed. "Okay. I'll try."

"Talk to her first. Then go see Great-Pop."

"All right," Autumn managed.

CHAPTER 27

"THANK YOU, Aunt Erin." She smiled at her aunt (who was really her mama's cousin). Erin was a lot younger than Mom and one of the cooler aunts Autumn had. She playfully punched Autumn's shoulder.

"Yeah, I know, I'm awesome."

"Best taxi service in the world!" Autumn agreed brightly and leaped out of her aunt's sleek red sports car. "Thank you!" she said again.

Then, backpack slung over her shoulder, she hurried up the wooden steps to the front porch and rang the doorbell. Aunt Erin waited until she saw Aunt Amy Jo open the front door before she drove off.

"Hi, Aunt Amy Jo." Autumn smiled at her. Amy Jo had been a teacher and then a librarian, and now she was a nurse, and she was really strict, especially when she thought people weren't listening to her. She made intense faces when she was displeased. Even at twelve, those faces still unnerved Autumn.

Once, when Autumn and some of the boys were running through the house at Christmas, she'd yelled at her and told her to act more like a lady. But she hadn't said a word to the boys, who went off in a pack in the other direction. Mama said Amy Jo was just nervous, because she'd been holding a carving knife when Autumn came around the corner first.

"She was scared she might have hurt you," Mama explained. "That's why she yelled."

But it stuck with Autumn, and she'd never really forgotten it.

"What are you doing here?" Aunt Amy Jo asked a bit abrasively.

"I'm here to see Great-Pop." And then remembering her mother's words she shifted and added, "And to visit with Great-Mom." This seemed to be the right answer, because Aunt Amy Jo stepped back and allowed her entry into the warm house. Something was cooking in the oven, and it smelled delicious.

"Why don't you leave your things in the hall and go wash up, and I'll tell Great-Mom you're here? I've just put the kettle on, but I bet you don't like tea, do you?"

Some of Emma's snarkiness rattled around in her brain. Her best friend would have said something sarcastic like, "I only drink it every time I come over here, but nah, I hate it." Mama had taught her better than that, though, and Autumn managed to be gracious.

"I could really use some tea right now."

Amy Jo laughed and went to the master bedroom to wake Great-Mom from her nap.

Autumn walked to the guest bathroom. It was decorated in the frilly pink, soft hues that were nothing like the sort of hot glittery pink that was Autumn's favorite color. It was subdued and faded. The sunlight that had shone through the bottom of the curtain for years had yellowed its hem. Autumn wondered if it had ever been pretty. She didn't think so.

Autumn fixed her windblown hair in the oval mirror with the gold angels at the top, and washed her hands with rich-smelling soap. She took a deep breath. She needed to be polite and pleasant and drink her tea as quickly as she could without being rude. And then she could go tell Great-Pop a story. Swallowing, she thought she knew which one needed telling.

Great-Mom was waiting for her at the table with a pleasant little smile that stretched out some of the wrinkles on her tired face. Aunt Amy Jo had fixed her white hair up into a top bun. Just getting up from a nap, she still managed to look elegant.

"Why, hello, Autumn," she said. She seemed genuinely pleased to see her, even though Autumn couldn't guess why. They never had anything to say to one another.

"Hi, Great-Mom," Autumn managed in reply. "How are you?"

"I'm a little tired," she said on an intake of breath, like she would muster through it for Autumn's sake, "but I'm well. Thank you for asking. Are you recovered from your illness?"

"Yes." She nodded. "I went to school today."

"That's wonderful."

Aunt Amy Jo placed tea bags in each of their cups. Great-Mom's was the delicate, fine china cup. Autumn's was a brown mug that looked like it had come from the dollar store. She stared at it as Amy Jo filled it with steaming hot water. She wasn't a baby. She wasn't going to break Great-Mom's precious china by drinking out of it, just like she wasn't going to break Great-Mom herself by giving her a hug.

"Do you want sugar?" Amy Jo asked.

"Yes, please," Autumn said flatly. One single sugar cube fell into her cup. Her expression must have betrayed her—that she thought a single cube wouldn't please an ant—because Amy Jo said sternly, "There's too much sugar in a child's diet these days."

And then she left them alone. For all of her faults, Aunt Amy Jo had, at least, been another body in the room. Someone to try to make conversation with. Now, it was just the two of them, alone in the kitchen, listening to the clock ticking off the seconds. Autumn smiled at her Great-Mom, a smile she wasn't really feeling, and looked back down into her cup.

Three more cubes of sugar broke the surface of the liquid, and she raised eyes to Great-Mom who whispered, "Amy Jo thinks there's too much sugar in an old lady's diet as well. But I think the tea is far too bitter without it."

Autumn's smile brightened just a touch.

"What did you do today, Great-Mom?"

"Mostly, I slept," she admitted. "But I also quilted until my arthritis started to flare, and then I read a little to Tom."

"You read to Great-Pop?" Autumn asked. "What are you reading?"

"The paper," she said. "Sad news and bad news everywhere, I'm afraid."

"You shouldn't do that." She realized a little too late how loud and rude she'd sounded, but how could Great-Mom think it was a good idea to read the paper to Great-Pop? If there was nothing but crime and murder and sad things written in there, then why would he ever want to wake up? Why would he want to come back to her? To any of them?

Great-Mom watched her levelly. "What do you suggest I read?"

"I don't know." Autumn shrugged. "Maybe the Bible. Maybe God will bring him back if you read him the Bible."

"That's a thought," Great-Mom said quietly.

"And nice stories. Better stories. Stories about friendship and love and good things. Summer days and… and sugar," she said, because her eyes landed on the small bowl with the daisy pattern around the rim.

"Yes, a very, very good point." Delicately, Great-Mom stirred her small spoon around in her tea and then laid it on her saucer. "I just thought, since Tom never missed the morning paper, that it was important to continue the tradition."

Autumn's heart skipped a beat, and she felt like a jerk for chastising Great-Mom.

"I'm… sorry," she managed and took a sip of her tea, even though it was still too hot. It burned her tongue.

"No, I'm sorry, Autumn," she said and very gently patted her hand. "I'm so sorry about your great-grandfather. I know how much he means to you. I hope you know that you're very special to Tom as well."

Autumn felt bad then. She should be the one comforting Great-Mom. He was her husband after all. But Autumn felt, selfishly, like she was the most important—or should be. Because she loved Great-Pop so very much, how could any of them possibly understand the way she felt? They finished their tea in silence, and when she'd gulped down the last drop, Autumn stood without even offering to help with the dishes and said, "I'm going to go visit him."

"All right," Great-Mom agreed.

Autumn sat silently in Great-Pop's room for a very long time. She knew what story she had to tell, but even though she was mad at Roy, she still didn't like it. She and Great-Pop were on a long drive when she asked Great-Pop what had happened to Roy, how he died. And Great-Pop had gotten really quiet, like he didn't want to share the story. But he did. It was the first time she'd ever seen her great-grandfather cry— even if it was just the one, silent tear.

CHAPTER 28

IT WAS late in the afternoon—nearing sunset. The sky was on fire with vibrant reds and oranges and the kind of vivid yellow that came only as the sun burned its way out of the day. They were having a picnic out in the orchard. It was Tommy's idea this time, and he'd spent most of the morning at the grocer and then preparing and packing up the meal. Neither one of them was much of a cook, but Roy said Tommy's soup could take the paint off a fence post.

"Well, you don't have to eat my cookin' then, do you?" Tommy said sourly.

"What kind of a wife can't even make dinner?"

"I'm not your wife." Tommy laughed, and they kissed. The food really was awful—even the sandwiches, and how exactly did a man go about screwing up a sandwich, Roy pointed out? The coffee was too strong, the blanket was torn, and he'd left the pie out to cool, then forgotten to pack it. The whole thing was a thrice-damned mess.

"Should've let my momma handle it."

"She does too much for us," Tommy said, "I've been thinking that maybe we should find somewhere else to live. Give her space, you know?"

"I've actually been thinking the same thing," Roy agreed. He'd lain out on the blanket and put his head into Tommy's lap, demanding playfully that Tommy rub his temple. "I think it's about time we go looking for something new."

"Yeah."

"We'll pack up the truck, and we'll start driving until we find the place we're meant to be," he said. "I've got something picked out."

"Oh yeah? You've been reading a map?" Tommy's temple rubs turned into light strokes, and then he was running his fingers through Roy's dark hair.

"Nah, nothing like that. I've just been imagining things. Maybe it isn't real. But I'd like for it to be. I'd like a place where nobody ever paid us no mind, and we could be together."

Tommy said, "We are together."

Crows had gathered nearby, eyeing their bread crusts. Tommy yipped, his best fox imitation, trying to scare them away, but Roy balled up the bread and chucked it to them. "Let 'em eat," he said. "I like crows."

"Crows and kids, huh?"

"Crows and kids," Roy agreed.

"Okay, so tell me about this place."

Roy's head was heavy in his lap, and he tapped his temple again. ("Right away, master," Tommy joked, and began his gentle headache massage once more.) "A cave, maybe? No, a valley, where no one would ever bother us, and we could do whatever we pleased. Something like this. Just you and me and the crows. The sun would never set except in this one part of the valley where it rains all the time."

"Sounds nice."

"It's more than nice. We can make love anytime, anywhere, any way we want, and we'll always be together and I'll rule the whole valley and keep everyone out."

"Won't that get boring?"

"Maybe. When we get bored, we'll make up friends, or we'll let people in. Until we're not bored and then we'll kick them out again."

Tommy laughed and leaned over and kissed Roy, lingering for a moment on the taste of his lips. "I think that sounds amazing. So where does the sun never set? Nevada? Colorado?"

"Farther," Roy told him. He was drowsy; his voice grew heavier, slower, distant. "Much, much farther."

"California, then," Tommy said, thinking there wasn't much west of there unless they flipped the map and ended up in China. He didn't think those guys would be any more keen on their love than the folks around here.

By the time he'd realized Roy was sleeping, Tommy was lost in thoughts about the future. He'd finished his glass of cheap red wine, so

he drank deeply out of Roy's abandoned glass and smiled. The place
Roy described, it was a fantasy—one of those fairy stories that mothers
told their children. A land of elves and dragons and such. But
somewhere else, a change for them? That was real. That was doable.
That was in their grasp. And packing up the truck and moving out of
Roy's Momma's house, that sounded real nice. Maybe they would have
to pretend to be brothers if they wanted to get a place to live, but he
didn't so much care about that. He just cared about being with Roy,
spending every day together, and the nights as well.

"So why is it that it never stops raining in that one side of the
valley?" Tommy asked playfully, after he'd drained his glass. It was
autumn, and the leaves had shed their green, revealing warm yellows,
fiery reds, and deep, unblemished oranges—the same colors as the
sunset. He should let Roy sleep, but he was starting to feel frisky again.
"Come on, wake up, sleepyhead." And he shook him. Roy's head lolled
to one side, but his eyes didn't open. "You're not fooling me again,
possum." Tommy shook him—harder.

"Roy?"

Another moment passed and he realized that Roy wasn't
breathing.

"Roy?"

The ambient sounds of the orchard fell away. Tommy could no
longer hear the crows or the gentle sound of the breeze through the
trees. There was only a pounding in his ears. With numb fingers, he
frantically searched Roy's chest for a heartbeat or the telltale rise and
fall of his ribcage, but there was nothing.

"Roy!"

His skin was still warm; he just wasn't moving, wasn't breathing.
There were no thoughts now, and thank Christ Tommy's body moved
without directions from his head, else he might have sat there with an
unresponsive Roy on his lap forever.

They were so damned far from the truck. Stupidly, Tommy stood,
rolling Roy out of his lap and onto his back on the blanket. He put his
hands on Roy's chest and began to push, trying to force life back into
him. "C'mon Roy, stop this!" He crouched down and lifted Roy's
heavy weight over his shoulder, heavier than two sacks of feed and half

as responsive, and he started to run—as well as he could run with that awkward burden—toward the truck, stumbling twice, ripping the knee out of his jeans. He couldn't feel pain, just the warm caress of blood trickling down his leg. "You're acting like a horse's ass, Roy! Stop it! Wake up!" He jostled him for good measure.

But Roy didn't revive.

Tommy tried to be gentle as he dumped Roy into the passenger side and dug in his pocket for the key. He was desperate for some sign of life, but there was no devil twinkling in Roy's eyes, no gotcha-grin. He was still, silent.

"You're ruinin' a perfectly good picnic, Roy." Words tumbled from his lips. He didn't even know what he was saying anymore. "My cooking isn't that bad."

Speeding down the highway, the gas pedal all the way to the floorboard, he at turns shouted and then whispered, all the while gripping Roy's hand hard enough to break the bones. At a hard bump, Roy fell forward into the dashboard and then slumped over onto Tommy's lap.

Dead weight.

Tommy was blinded by his sudden tears.

He slowed—cars behind him honking—and pulled Roy's truck over onto the shoulder, put it in park, and sat while the evening traffic passed him by. For a long time that was the only sound, cars speeding busily home.

Looking down at Roy, he reached out and very gently touched his beautiful face. Roy was dead.

AFTER THE service and the burial, when all the casserole dishes were returned and it was just he and Roy's Momma alone in her house, she took his hand and asked, "Why?" Twenty or thirty times a day she asked. Why? Why? *Why?* Healthy, twenty-two year old men didn't just die for no reason.

She went a little mad then. She stopped cleaning and cooking, she stopped going to church, and she insisted Tommy stay near her all the time. She wanted him close so he could tell her again, a million times over, what had happened. She was blind to Tommy's pain. She just wanted answers, as if answers would make her hurting stop.

Tommy had made up a story, because he couldn't tell her the truth—the way they'd made love on that blanket before they'd had dinner. In the version he invented, they were going bowling, and Roy just collapsed outside the alley. He could say that they were at home when it happened because Roy's Momma had been out visiting a neighbor who had just had a baby.

She wanted to know what Roy was wearing when it happened, what he said, how he looked, how he sounded. She didn't seem to notice when the details changed just a little each time—it was like she was hearing it all for the first time anyway.

"Just collapsed," she repeated, her eyes unseeing. She bit her fingernails until they were bloody stumps. "Healthy, twenty-two year old boys don't just die for no reason," she whispered to her checkered tablecloth. "My baby."

Autopsy said he'd had an aneurism. Gone in a second. Painless. All those headaches and headache powders? The signs were there. Something was wrong—always had been. Medically there was a reason—but in the grand scheme of love and life? Tommy agreed with Roy's mother. It was pointless. It was a waste. It was a plot in a dime novel. It was shit. And above all, it just wasn't fair. Roy hadn't been reckless or wild or asking for it. He'd just been lying there, head in Tommy's lap, thinking about the future. And then he was gone. It was fate's cruelest joke.

CHAPTER 29

AUTUMN REALIZED she'd run out of things to say about the story because that was all Great-Pop had ever told her, other than that Roy's Momma eventually passed away. She knew from Roy that seven years later Tommy married Virginia and took on her children as his own. But what happened during the in-between years? Did he move away from town? What did he do for work? Where did he go? She just didn't know.

What she did know was Great-Pop had not stirred once during her whole story.

"Don't you understand the point, Great-Pop?" she asked, her knees up under her chin in the little side chair. "Roy left a long time ago. He left over fifty years ago. He's gone. But we're still here. Great-Mom and all your kids and grandkids and great-grandkids. *Me*, Great-Pop. I'm here. Everyone misses you and wishes you would wake up."

She sniffed and rubbed one eye with her palm. "He left you, Great-Pop. He doesn't deserve your time or your heart."

AUTUMN TRIED to be cheerful at dinner when she met Mama's friend Jack, but it was difficult. For one thing, he wasn't anything like she'd imagined. With the name Jack, she expected Jack Phineas, the handsome actor, with his piercing green eyes and his charming smile. But Mama's Jack was a bit heavy, and even though he'd shaved his hair down to a fine fuzz, it was obvious he was going bald. She wouldn't tell Mama, of course, especially not with the way Mama smiled at him like he really was as handsome as Jack Phineas—but Autumn didn't think he was cute at all.

He did bring her mama flowers though, and he gave Autumn a stuffed panda bear holding a baby bear in its paws. Emma would have scoffed and asked him what did he think she was? Five? And it was a pretty childish gift—but secretly Autumn still kept stuffed animals in her closet, way at the back. She'd never have put them out or anything, but she liked the panda. She called it Didi. Looking up, she caught her mother smiling conspiratorially at Jack.

Autumn tried her best to stay focused on what was happening— the dinner and the bear and the conversation—but she kept going spacey. Her plans for getting Great-Pop back just weren't working. He was still in his coma, and nothing she did seemed to have the slightest effect.

She had to try again tonight to go to the valley, but what good would that do her if she had no control over her body? It was time to amp things up.

"Should we play a game?" Mama asked brightly, after everyone—except Autumn—had cleaned their plates. She tried, but her stomach wasn't into it. Mama gave her a pass, this one time. Maybe because she'd been sick. Maybe because Mama didn't want to fight in front of Jack.

They played Monopoly. Autumn was the little dog, and Mama was the top hat, and Jack was the sports car. It was pretty fun, all things considered. They talked together, and Jack asked a ton of questions. He also answered all of hers, which impressed her. What did he do? He was a manager at a textiles factory. Was that boring? Autumn! Yes, just a little, but it paid well enough that he could keep sending money to his daughter every month. He had a daughter? Had he been married before? Yes, her name was Clara, but no, he hadn't married her mother. She was sixteen and pretty. He didn't like the boy she was dating. Autumn liked how honest and open he seemed, never flinching from any of her questions as they moved their pieces around the board.

"Do you like my mama?" Autumn asked as she landed on Free Parking and—by house rules—inherited all of the bail money that Mama, jailbird that she was, had contributed to the pot. She did not count it gleefully, as she had the last time she landed there. She simply stared at their guest and waited for his answer.

Jack looked at her levelly for a moment and then smiled. "Yes, I really do."

"All right then." Autumn passed the dice to him.

That night she tried praying again before she went to sleep. She asked that God allow her back into the valley and that she have control over her legs and her mouth and her brain, if nothing else. She didn't suppose she'd really need her arms. But then at the last minute, she thought, how was she to open doors? Especially if Red-Eye guarded them and tried to force her to practice her lessons and such? Or, if her arms betrayed her and grabbed onto the molded paneling in the walls as her legs tried to move her forward. She amended the prayer, and asked again, this time for every part of herself.

"I'm going to tell Great-Pop exactly how to get home," she promised God and then tried to fall asleep. It was a long while before it finally overtook her, eager expectation keeping her more awake than normal. But when she did finally drift off, it was not the valley that she returned to, but a distorted nightmare.

THERE WAS a sign, huge and looming, that said Sunset Valley, population: Rain King, but it looked like downtown, and it wasn't sunset; it was midday. All the people around her were really tall. No, that wasn't right. She was really short. She couldn't reach door handles, or ledges even, to hoist herself up. And all she could think was that she had to get to Great-Pop. But she didn't know where he was. She reached out for the folks in their business suits walking past her to work, but they ignored her. Or, when they didn't, her throat dried up, and she could barely whisper what she needed. As she walked around the same city block, over and over again, she grew by degrees, until she was tall enough that she could reach a cell phone that a woman held out to her. At first, nothing happened when she dialed, but then a woman's voice asked her if she needed assistance. The voice on the other end of the phone sounded very far away, and her words were difficult to make out.

"I'm trying to reach my Great-Pop," Autumn explained. "His name is Tom Johnson. I'd like to speak to him."

The woman on the other end of the line was silent, and then there were a few clicks and the dial tone came on. Autumn started to push the buttons she thought were the right numbers to call, but they kept jumping around on her, and she would have to hang up and try again.

No matter what she did, she couldn't get the number to dial correctly. And then it started to ring, and an angry sounding man answered.

"Who is this? What do you want?"

"I want to speak to Great-Pop," she said. "Is he there?"

"He's here. You can't talk to him. We all hate you. Go away!"

"No, wait," she begged. She couldn't seem to put any emotion into her voice. "I would really like to talk to my Great-Pop. I need to let him know something."

"I'll tell him," the angry sounding man said.

"No, you won't," she argued, because she somehow knew that he wouldn't. She didn't believe he was even there with Great-Pop. She turned, and she was in her living room holding the house phone, and there was a dial tone. There were no buttons on the receiver and none on the face of the phone. She hung up. How was she supposed to reach Great-Pop if she couldn't call?

She could go over to his house! She would tell him a story. She would shake him and tell him a story at the same time, and he would wake up. She put on her parka and her backpack, but she forgot her pants and kept having to pull the end of her parka down so no one would see her panties outside. She ran down a really, really long dirt road. And for every running step, she kicked a crow, and it went flying through the air, squawking expletives at her.

Daddy was waiting for her at the stop sign. He told her, "Great-Mom is dead."

"Great-Mom?" she repeated, disbelieving.

"No, I mean Great-Pop. Great-Pop is dead."

"You're lying!" she shouted.

"Would I lie to you?" And he pulled his face off like a mask, and behind it was a black-and-white version of Roy with a cruel smile and crueler eyes. And he started to laugh at her. He bent right over and laughed in her face, and she started to hit him, but her arms were weak. Even though her fists hit him right in the nose and mouth and eyes, she was doing no damage. She exerted all her efforts trying to beat him down, and she grew weaker and weaker until there was nothing left but tears. She sank down in the middle of nowhere, defeated.

CHAPTER 30

AUTUMN SHOT up in bed, silent tears of frustration streaming down her face, her body chilled with sweat. She yanked the covers off and flung them to the floor. And then she grabbed the panda she'd been sleeping with and flung that. And then her pillows, one after another, until it was just her, alone on the mattress. She sat there, breathing heavily, hugging herself. It wasn't working. It wasn't working! She hadn't gone to the valley at all, not even as a puppet!

She was tired, but not tired enough. That was the problem—she wasn't tired the way she'd been when she first got sick. She didn't sleep so deep that when she woke up her mouth was a desert and her body was stiff from lying in the same, unmoved position. If she could sleep—*really sleep*—then she could go back there and tell Great-Pop everything. She would have control over her body, and she would find the valley again, and there was no way she would get pulled out before she was ready.

Slowly, Autumn swung her shaky legs over the side of the bed and put her bare feet into the lush carpet. There was a bottle of pills that Mama kept in the cabinet for the nights when she was having a difficult time going to sleep. The doctor gave them to her after Daddy left. She used to take them a lot. She didn't take them so much anymore. If she could just take a couple of those, then she could go back into a deep sleep.

Autumn had to stand on the footstool to reach the top of the cabinet, and it creaked when she opened it. She didn't want to wake Mama up. In the whole kitchen there were two cabinets she was supposed to stay out of. The medicine cabinet where Mama kept her prescriptions and the bottom cabinet where all the alcohol was. Sometimes she and Emma would open up the bottom cabinet and look at the bottles. One time they took sips out of the gin and got red-faced and laughed at everything. They probably weren't even drunk, just excited by breaking the rules. Truth was, she didn't really like the taste of alcohol.

It took her a few tries, pulling down the wrong bottles: antacid, aspirin, and a prescription she didn't recognize, and then finally she found the little brown bottle. The name didn't mean much to her, but she recognized the shape of the green pills, and the warning label said not to operate heavy machinery.

"I won't," she promised quietly.

Autumn got herself a glass of water and opened the bottle. The instructions said to take no more than one in a twenty-four hour period. But she needed them to work quickly, and she needed them to work well. Sometimes, when Mama was having a really bad migraine, she would take four aspirin even though the bottle said not to. This never seemed to do her much harm, so Autumn decided four was a good number of pills. She had to take them one at a time, because she still didn't like swallowing pills and hadn't learned yet how to pop them all in her mouth and swallow the way Great-Pop did. He could take six pills at a time, depending on how big they were. She was really impressed with that, especially because until she was eight, Mama had to open her capsules up and pour them over ice cream for her. She finished her water and put the glass in the sink, and then she waited. They weren't doing anything.

Autumn wasn't dumb. She knew what she was doing with Mama's pills was wrong and possibly dangerous, but this was, *literally*, a matter of life or death. She poured another glass and counted out another four pills. She needed them to work *quickly*.

Back in her bedroom, she lay under the covers and stared up at the ceiling for a very long time, wondering how long it was supposed to take for her to get sleepy. And then it hit her, and she was suddenly very, very lightheaded. This made her smile. It was working!

She snuggled down and readied herself for the valley. She was going to take Toren's hand and tell him, "I'm your great-granddaughter, Autumn."

"Autumn." The second voice that spoke her name aloud was not her own. She opened one eye as best she could. Roy was standing there, and he did not look pleased.

"I'm coming for you," she warned him drowsily.

"No, you aren't, Autumn. You've done something very, very bad," he said. But it was the way he said it. He wasn't challenging her.

"You're just worried...." she said. All her words were sticking in her throat, and when she managed to force them out, they hung for a long time. It was difficult to vocalize her thoughts. Her head was fuzzy. "I'm going to tell him how to get back here. And he's going to... leave you...."

"Autumn." Roy bent low over her, so their faces were mere inches apart. His eyes, which were always so coldly blue, were now shimmering with concern. "Listen to me, all right? Tommy would never forgive me if I didn't try to help you, you stupid little girl. You've done something bad. Get out of bed, and go tell your mother."

"I'm sleepy," Autumn moaned, pushing at him with her weak might. It was just like the dream, when she tried to fight him off and her punches were like feathers against his face. "I don't want... Great-Pop... to die...."

"Sit up," he commanded. "Sit up, or it will be *you* that dies, Autumn. Put your feet on the floor. Let's go get your mother."

"You get her," she grumbled.

"I *can't* get her. She *can't* see me."

"You just want...."

"I just want what your Great-Pop wants, Autumn. I want you to grow up and live your life and make mistakes and be ridiculous and fall in love and have an amazing time doing it. Autumn!"

She forced her eyes open. He was so loud. Why was he so loud? Didn't he know that she was trying to go to sleep? Didn't he know she had things she needed to do?

"I will send him back to you, if you go tell your mother what you've done." His voice was like marble and she blinked, barely comprehending.

"You'll... let me have him?"

"Yes," he whispered, brushing sweaty pieces of hair out of her face. They didn't really move, of course, but it felt comforting, nonetheless. "Because I love him. And he loves you. Put your feet on the floor."

The whole room jerked violently to one side, and Autumn's legs gave out when she tried to stand. But Roy, above her, barked that she needed to keep moving. That he wouldn't release Great-Pop if she didn't make it to Mama's room. So she crawled, on hands and knees that felt like they were made of iron. She crawled across the carpeted hallway, into the kitchen, dragging herself over the linoleum. She knocked into a chair and almost collapsed, but he kept at her like a drill sergeant, telling her where to move and how to put her body so she would make it. And finally, she felt the metal rim between the kitchen floor and the bedroom carpet, and she collapsed across it, like she'd run a marathon.

"Call out," Roy demanded, but her lips wouldn't move, and her throat was tight. It was the dream. This was another nightmare. "Call *out!*" he insisted desperately. Instead, Autumn reached with her last little bit of strength, and she grabbed one of the swinging brass handles on Mama's side table and began to rhythmically tap with it until she lost all consciousness.

CHAPTER 31

IT WAS so bright that she struggled to see anything at all.

Every way she turned, eyes up, eyes down, all around her, close or far in the distance (which was actually impossible to gauge) there was nothing but the brilliant white. Focusing on her pale hands first and then her feet, she started to move, slowly, because she couldn't feel anything underneath her. When she reached out to steady herself, she found nothing to grab on to and tumbled forward. She spilled into more nothing, into light. She could fall or not fall. She was and she wasn't.

She could make herself breathe, but she didn't need to. She could make herself blink, but her eyes weren't dry or tired. In fact, she almost could not feel herself at all. She had to focus on what she remembered, what skin upon skin felt like, to feel her hands touching each other, and then when she linked them, she had to force herself to remember pressure and warmth. She was not scared. She was not anything.

She continued to move forward.

The light was less painful as she grew accustomed to it, but still there was nothing to see. The bright light was formless. It was everywhere. It was nowhere. She lay down, even though she did not feel tired, and when she stood and moved, she could not tell if she was moving quickly or slowly or not at all. There was nothing to compare her speed to relatively. There was nothing to head toward, or run away from, or move past.

She climbed up, as she imagined "Up" to be. She used an unnecessary swimming stroke, because she wanted to do it. Because she thought it would be fun. And that was her first real desire in this bright white place. She wanted to swim. And then all of a sudden, swimming was possible, and she was swimming fluidly through the white, moving forward and up and down and any which way. And she knew her directions because she could see a tiny speck of something that wasn't bright and wasn't white. A hint of color in the very far-off distance. She wanted to move closer to it, so she did. She swam and leaped and ran toward it and focused on it.

By the time the speck had form, her heart had fully enveloped another wish, a wish much larger and grander than the desire to swim or to know what was up and what was down. It was a bigger wish, even, than wanting to reach the speck. She wanted the speck to be Great-Pop. She wanted to be where Great-Pop was.

One more step and she was there, even though he'd seemed so far away just a moment before. He was sitting, his old face lined and tired, his eyes blank, a slightly bemused smile curving his lips She knelt down beside him in the nothing and put her hand on his hand. She remembered what it felt like, and she felt it then.

"Great-Pop," she whispered. "I found you."

For a long time he didn't move, didn't speak, didn't blink.

"Please talk with me, Great-Pop. I've been waiting so long."

Slowly he turned his head, and he took her features in, and recognition entered those dark eyes.

"Autumn," he breathed.

She threw her arms around him and hugged him for minutes and hours and days. She hugged him and hugged him and felt such fulfillment for having reached him, finally.

"What are you doing here?" he asked. "This place isn't for you."

"I've come to take you home," she said. "I've come to get you out of the valley." She looked around. This bright place, this empty, white expanse, it wasn't the valley at all. There were no hills or gardens, no forest, no animals, no sunsets, no rain, no cottage, and no castle. There was no Rook, and Great-Pop was not Toren. There was no Roy, and something was strange about this Tommy. This place was somewhere else; it was nothing and everything.

"Where are we?" she asked quietly.

"Waiting."

"Waiting?" she asked. "Where is that?"

"That is waiting." His tone had not changed. He looked pleasant. He looked right through her. It was nothing like talking to Toren, who flared with passion and yelled and smiled and laughed and sometimes cried. And it was nothing like talking to Great-Pop when he would tell her all the amazing stories about his past.

"Let's go back home," she insisted, lacing her fingers in his. "I would like to go back home. With you." She did not notice it immediately, because the change was so very subtle, but once she had spoken those words, the brightness around them dimmed by degrees.

"All right. We can go when we're done waiting."

"I don't understand," Autumn argued. "What are we waiting for?"

"We're just waiting."

This reply frustrated her when before she had felt nothing but fulfillment. Waiting? Why didn't he get to *wanting*? She'd wanted almost immediately, and it had her swimming. Wanting had her feeling, wanting had her finding him here.

"Don't you *want* to come home with me?" she cried. "Don't you *want* to wake up?"

For a moment he just stared at her, and then he reached out and touched her young face. "Why can't I feel you?" he asked. "I thought I heard you whispering. So I sat down here and I started to wait. But why can't I feel you, Autumn?"

"Because you… you don't *want* to!" she exclaimed. The brightness was growing duller by the second.

"I remember being so tired. And then I wasn't. I'm not tired here."

"You're not anything here! You're not happy! You're—waiting!" she exclaimed. "You're waiting, Great-Pop! For nothing and no one and never!"

She noticed then that the brightness was now full of forms and colors. "Great-Pop, c'mon, get up! Let's go! You *want* to go. You *want* to come home to me."

Great-Pop just looked at her, unblinking. All around them, the nothing was starting to turn, to become solid. She couldn't make out the features, but she didn't care because as the bright became darker, Great-Pop became lighter, fuzzier, more out of focus. She was losing him, and no matter how much she trained her heart and her love on him, she couldn't make him stay.

"Great-Pop? Why? Is it Roy you want? Do you want to be with him instead?"

He blinked very, very slowly and whispered, "Roy?"

Her heart was heavy, and she'd lost all feelings of warmth and comfort and fulfillment. She could feel solid ground underneath her now. She could not swim up and down, and the light was almost completely gone. Great-Pop had almost completely faded.

"Do you want to go to see Roy?" she asked, taking his hand and pulling it to her. She was going to hold it until it wasn't there anymore, until he was completely gone. "Do you want to go to where Roy is? Great-Pop?"

Again, for just a second, his eyes seemed to focus.

"I would rather he have you than see you like this!" She kissed his old, scarred knuckles and held his hand to her cheek and cried, shutting her eyes tightly. "I'll get you to Roy, I promise. *I promise!* Just put it in your heart. Want it. You don't have to wait anymore."

CHAPTER 32

WHEN AUTUMN'S eyes finally opened, they were tired and gritty, and her lids felt heavy. Somehow she knew she was in a hospital room, even though it looked nothing like Great-Pop's and even less like the ones in the movies. She was lying on a small, hard bed with high metal railings, and stiff blankets were tucked tightly around her legs and stomach. The whole room was dim, with only running lights above the headboard to illuminate the space. Mama was asleep in a chair beside her, using her arms like a pillow against the uncomfortable-looking armrests. Roy was right. She had done something real bad. Her eyes dragged closed again, and she whispered hoarsely, "Roy? Roy are you there?"

Her throat was so sore she could barely swallow. For a time she lay there, listening to the muffled sounds of people farther down the hall. That was one good thing about her room—she didn't have Great-Pop's angry hospital roommate to yell at her for making noise.

"Mama?" she tried, but Mama was out. Autumn started to reach for her mother when she heard Roy, quiet, nearby.

"I'm here," he said finally.

"Have you been here the whole time?" she asked, turning toward the sound of his voice. She could see him, shadowed in the corner. A tiny, fragmented memory of their last conversation came to her. "Great-Pop! In the valley! You didn't let him go yet, did you?"

"Not yet," he said stiffly. "But I will. I promised you I—"

"No, no, no," she begged. "Please no, please don't let him go. Hold on to him with everything you've got." Her voice came out in a tiny rasp. Her throat became more raw with every word, and it was getting difficult to speak, but she had to tell him. "I saw him. He was… waiting. He wasn't happy. He wasn't anything. I don't want him to be like that anymore. I don't want him to wait anymore."

"Autumn," Roy said quietly, right next to her ear. "I am sorry. What an ass I've been, arguing and fighting with a little girl. I just lost myself. I've missed him for so long."

She forced her gritty eyes open just a crack and looked right into his bright blue ones. "You're the one he wants, Roy. I thought it was me. But it was you."

"He wants us both, princess. And that's why he's stuck. That's why he hasn't woken up for you, and why he can't remember himself when he's in the valley with me."

"Roy? If I let him go...." She couldn't speak anymore, she was too tired, her throat hurt too much, but really, it was just too difficult to say out loud. So she lay there and steadied her breathing. She thought as loud as she could think and hoped he could hear her. *If I let him go, will you promise me you'll take care of him?*

She didn't hear his answer. She'd lost herself back to the medicine the hospital had given her.

MAMA WAS really quiet on the car ride home. She kept reaching out and touching Autumn's hair or her cheek or squeezing her leg, but all the while her gaze was fixed on the road. She was pretending not to cry, again. This time, though, Autumn reached out and put her hand on her mother's arm and did her best to comfort her.

"I'm sorry, Mama," she said as clearly as she could. Her words broke her mother's resolve, and she started to sob so hard she had to pull off the road until she could get control over herself.

"I-I don't understand." Mama cried, wailing like a little girl who had just broken her favorite doll. "You're... you're only twelve. How can you possibly be...?"

Autumn didn't understand. She said she was sorry again. She hadn't explained why she'd done it. She'd gone about it wrong, even if she had finally reached the place where Great-Pop was.

"Mama?" she asked.

"Is it because I-I brought Jack home?" She turned toward Autumn, her face a wet mess. Mama didn't look pretty when she cried.

"No. No, I like Jack!" she assured her. "I really like Jack! I just—" Autumn took in a sharp breath. "I just wanted to go to sleep, and I was having trouble, and I remembered that you had some pills to help you sleep and—"

Her mother let loose a long wail and fell against the steering wheel, her shoulders shaking with sobs. "It's my fault, it's my fault."

"No, Mama. I'm sorry! I didn't take 'em right."

"It's too much pressure. The divorce and a new boyfriend and Granddaddy. It's too much pressure."

Cars flew past them on the road, their drivers oblivious to the way Mama cried. They had places to be, their own families, their own concerns. Autumn looked at her mother, and asked, "Do you mean yourself, or do you mean me?"

"W-what?"

"Too much pressure. Do you mean on yourself or me?"

And Mama gathered her to her chest, and she cried and cried and cried.

"Mama?" Autumn asked, trying her best hand at soothing. She wiped her mother's face inexpertly with her sleeve and pushed back the bits of her hair that stuck around her eyes and her runny nose. "We'll get through it together. All of it."

"Baby-doll, did you want to die when you took those pills?"

Autumn blinked, her brow knit in confusion, and then she blinked again and again and then suddenly, it bubbled up inside of her; laughter. Real, honest to God laughter. She hadn't laughed like this in so long, and once it started, the hilarity that her mother thought—! She laughed until her sides began to hurt, and she rolled away from Mama into the passenger side door, and she laughed until tears sprang into her eyes.

Mama, however, did not think it was funny, and she snapped, "Well?"

"No!" Autumn exclaimed. "No, no, no, Mama, I just wanted to sleep, and I did it all wrong. Kill myself?" It caught in her throat. She didn't know why she thought that was so funny, but she did and Lord, she laughed. When finally she got control of herself, she said something her mother had said to her once. "I don't have time to be dead."

It was almost imperceptible, but Mama's lips quirked.

"I need you to stay out of my medicine cabinet."

"I will," Autumn agreed solemnly.

"I need you to promise it. No, I need you to *swear* it."

"Are you sure? You got kinda angry the last time I swore."

"Just this once, ignore what I said and listen to what I'm saying. Autumn, *swear to me* that you won't ever go into my medicine cabinet again."

"I capital S Swear, Mama." She leaned her head against her mother's arm.

"All right then," Mama said and put the car back into motion. When they were almost to the house she said, "When we have our follow-up with the doctor, you've got to tell them exactly what you just told me."

A follow-up. Of course there would be one if they really thought she'd been trying to kill herself.

"Okay."

"Do you want to go visit Great-Mom and Great-Pop?"

Autumn bit her lip and closed her eyes very, very tight.

CHAPTER 33

The rain smelled sweeter than ever that evening. Gone was the quiet drizzle, and in its place a downpour swept across the whole of the lands. Toren watched it from his seat at the window and thought about the little waterfall and the creek. It would flood and send water spreading all over the forest floor. How many times had it flooded? How often had the sunset rays dried it up?

He felt Rook behind him before he heard him, and then his image was in the glass. A rain-streaked, distorted reflection. Toren smiled in spite of himself; he was a man nearing defeat, and he thought he might be okay with that.

"Hello," Rook said quietly. His voice was slightly pensive that evening.

"I've been wondering," Toren said in way of a reply, "if you settled in the Rain Kingdom because it's so beautiful here or if it's because of something else?"

"I couldn't handle the sunset without you." He said this so briskly that Toren almost thought it was a joke. Toren tapped his knuckle against the glass. There was something hypnotizing about the rain—it made him miss the cottage less, and it lulled him. Or maybe that was just Rook.

"I'm going to end up giving in to you, I'm afraid," Toren told him. His breath fogged the cold glass for a moment before dissipating.

"You make it sound horrible." Rook's expression was inscrutable, but his eyes were intense on Toren's reflection. "But it doesn't matter. I've got other plans in the works. Something your lovely Reina has devised for us."

Toren turned to him then, one arm on his knee. "You've seen Reina? Where is she?"

"Home," Rook replied. "Home. Safe. Not happy, not yet, but she will be."

"Are you saying she's not ever coming back?"

"That's not it," he said and moved slowly, fully, into the room. "You know, I've thought so many times about how to get you in my arms once I realized you were here. I could have just taken you, you know?"

"You've made it abundantly clear that you think so," Toren said dryly. "Though I don't know about that. I was out-armed last time. Give me a sword next time and we'll see." He chuckled and leaned his head forward against the cool windowpane. "Why didn't you try it if you were so certain of your victory?"

"I guess I'm just sappy."

"The master of the Rain Kingdom? Sappy? Doubtful."

"I never let it show back then, and I certainly won't now. But yes, sappy. Sentimental even."

Rook sat down on the rug near one of the six serene pools and beckoned for Toren to join him. He moved away from his seat at the window and took a spot near enough to Rook that they could touch. He wanted to touch.

Through the painfully clear water, Toren could see where a copper drain led down and out of the room to keep the little pool from overflowing, no matter how heavy the downpour. It was a brilliant design. The whole castle, the whole kingdom. He had, despite himself, come to truly appreciate it.

"I have a confession to make to you," Rook said, toying with one of Toren's curls. He pulled gently and let it spring back into place.

"Oh?"

Rook leaned in and kissed Toren's ear. Whispering huskily, he admitted, "I don't know that you would have gotten your memories back at all even if you had allowed me to make love to you."

Somehow, this brazen admission only made Toren laugh quietly—maybe because he'd felt it when they'd kissed, the memories stirring. He turned and looked Rook right in the eye, saying, "I've told you that I've been considering my own defeat, and not only do you not throw me down on the mattress and rip my clothes off my body, but you give away your hand. You're no rakehell at all."

"No." Rook moved his kiss to Toren's mouth. "No, I think not."

"So what stays your hands? The plan Reina has devised?"

"I've never wanted anyone but *you*. The *real* you. The you that you don't yet remember." Rook nuzzled Toren gently. "We'll know when it's time. And while there won't be any need for shirt ripping, I'm certain I will perpetrate it, regardless. It's been a long time, after all."

Toren flushed despite himself and leaned into Rook just a little. "Well, while we're waiting...."

"Yes?"

"I want to know more about this valley."

"All right. Ask and I will cryptically answer, just to bother you."

Toren stifled a laugh. "Well, you can start by telling me why your damned crow has one red eye."

Rook thought about this for a long while. He put his fingers into the rain pool and trailed patterns there as he mused over the answer. Or perhaps, as he'd intimated, he was simply trying to annoy Toren with his delay. When he finally spoke, the answer was far from satisfying. "Because fifty years is a very long time."

"That's definitely not an answer," Toren argued. But at Rook's steady gaze, he said, "Or, it's not one that I understand at least!"

"You *don't* understand," Rook agreed, standing up and stretching. "Wash up, join me for dinner. It may well be the last stiff and formal dinner as 'enemies' that we'll have to endure."

"Wait!" Toren demanded from his spot on the floor "Seriously, what about fifty years makes your bird's eye red?"

"Fifty years is a long time. A long, boring, lonely, miserable time. And I passed the days and hours and minutes and seconds making this space for you. Everything here is for you." When he could see Toren was still confused, he beckoned him up off the ground. "Her eye is red for you and because of you. I made details to make details. I made details so I didn't go crazy waiting for you."

CHAPTER 34

AUTUMN HAD tea with Great-Mom first. Not because her mother asked her to and not because she suddenly had anything more to say to her, but because she knew this visit with Great-Pop would be her very last. Aunt Amy Jo poured the tea, Autumn's in her dumb mug and Great-Mom's in her teacup, and then she left them alone to not speak to one another.

Autumn looked down into her mug and wished she knew what to say to Great-Mom. She wished she knew how to ask Great-Mom about stories from her own life. She might not be the storyteller Great-Pop was, but surely she had *something* interesting to say? In this, Autumn could delay what needed doing with Great-Pop. And also, maybe, her great-grandmother deserved good company. She just didn't know how to make the words come.

The sound of the chair scraping against the kitchen floor startled Autumn, and she looked up to see Great-Mom walking toward the glass china cabinet she kept in the hall.

"Great-Mom?"

"It's silly, Autumn, that a young woman shouldn't be allowed to drink out of her own teacup. I was a lot younger than you when my mother took me to my first high tea."

Taking the key to the cabinet off the top where it lay—unhidden—Great-Mom turned it in the lock and removed one of the small cups Autumn had so long coveted. When Great-Mom set the cup and saucer down on the table in front of her, Autumn had to swallow hard to get the lump out of her throat. She poured the tea out of her mug and into the cup.

"It's beautiful," she whispered.

"Tom bought me this set when we were first married," she said with a smile. "He broke a cup not too long after."

"Great-Pop broke a cup?"

"Oh, yes. He wasn't allowed to use my china after that."

Autumn laughed despite herself, imagining her gentle great-grandfather fumbling with the delicate china and sweet, proper Great-Mom forbidding him from touching any other piece.

"Great-Mom?" Autumn asked after a very long time sipping at the delicate edge of the cup. "Do you know where Great-Pop keeps his treasures?"

"His treasures?"

"Things that are important to him. You know how Aunt Vivian has all that junk in her cedar chest? Like letters and christening gowns and stuff like that? Does Great-Pop have anything like that?"

"Not a cedar chest, no," Great-Mom said, "but he does keep a cigar box of old things in our closet. This and that. Knick-knacks, really."

"Is there a chess piece in there?"

"I'm not at all certain, Autumn. It's been a long time since he had it down and even longer since I looked inside it with him," Great-Mom said. "You're welcome to look for yourself if you'd like. Is there a particular reason you're looking for a chess piece?"

"I… don't know," she lied with a half shrug. It was a bad lie, given that she'd brought it up out of nowhere. "I guess he just told me about it once. I can't remember. I thought I would put it beside his bed."

They'd been so close to talking too, but this was about Great-Pop and what Autumn needed to do. She couldn't help Great-Mom now.

THE CLOSET was neatly organized with Great-Pop's shirts and pants and shoes on the one side and Great-Mom's dresses hanging on the other. Along the top shelf were several hatboxes and mason jars full of change and a lock-box and there, right at the end, the worn cigar box.

"There's a footstool under his blazers," Great-Mom said, standing in the doorway. Autumn found it and used it to reach the box. She expected to pull down a layer of dust along with the box, but it was clean, like it had been recently opened. They took it into the kitchen and with only mild trepidation, Autumn pulled back the lid.

She expected to see a slew of boyhood trinkets—something befitting the cigar box—but inside there were only two things. The rook from his stories and a dried rose with a bow. Autumn touched one of the browned petals and it crumbled under her fingertips. Then she grabbed the rook and held it in her hand. There were spots where the varnish was worn thin. Autumn imagined that first year after Roy died. Did Great-Pop clutch the rook so tightly and caress it so much that he wore the varnish off?

She expected Great-Mom to ask her more about it, but as Autumn turned the worn rook between her fingertips, Great-Mom just pulled the box over to her.

"This is the rose I gave him on our first anniversary."

Autumn looked at the sad brown flower. "You remember? I mean… that was a long time ago."

"See this ribbon?" She pointed at the double-bowed ribbon around the stem. Great-Mom smiled. "I tied this ribbon. I can't believe that Tom kept it."

Autumn could. He'd kept it in the box with his rook—because it may not have been a romantic love he'd felt for Great-Mom, but it was a love nonetheless. She was his best friend in the whole world, his companion. He'd spent more than fifty years with her. She was every bit as important as Roy, just in a different way.

Slowly Great-Mom laid the flower back into the box, somehow managing not to damage a single petal.

"Thank you, Autumn," she said, "for visiting him."

CHAPTER 35

ALONE WITH him in his room, Autumn watched her great-grandfather for a long time. Great-Pop looked, as he always did these days, like he was just sleeping. She knew now that there was no noise loud enough to wake him from the place he was. Silently she kicked off her shoes, and with no thought about it, she climbed right up into bed next to him. She wrapped her arms around him and hugged him as tightly as she could manage. She was crying already, and she hadn't even found her words yet. They stuck in her throat and everything inside of her fought against doing it. But she stretched up and kissed his unshaven cheek and whispered in his ear, "Great-Pop? It's Autumn."

Of course he made no movement, no sign that he heard her, but she had faith that he knew she was there beside him. "Great-Pop? I tried so hard to bring you back. I'm sorry. I'm so, so sorry."

She was the reason he'd been hanging on for so long, caught in between worlds. She was the one who had been selfish, who had wanted him to stay even though it was his time. She was scared of a world without him in it.

"I know you're tired." She nuzzled his cheek, hot tears spilling from her eyes, rolling down her cheeks and nose, catching on her chin. "I love you so much and I don't want you to go away. I'm going to miss you."

Her words escaped in a shuddering sob.

"I'm going to miss you, so, so, so much." She squeezed him tighter. "But... you can...." All the words failed her. And she held him and cried. She cried so long and so loud that Aunt Amy Jo came to the door to check on her.

"He's fine!" she sobbed. "Go away! Go away!"

She was saying her good-byes, and she wanted privacy. After Aunt Amy Jo had assured herself that he was, indeed, still breathing, she quietly shut the door, understanding, maybe, what it was Autumn was trying to do.

"Great-Pop? Do you remember our tree-guessing game? You're so good at it and... I'm sorry, I hate trees." She half laughed and half cried. "But I love you, and I like that you love trees. So I played. But I didn't really care."

She sniffed hard and felt snot go down her throat.

"Great-Pop....

"I've got to say good-bye now.

"I don't want to. But I don't think you're happy like this. I don't think it's good that you're caught here, like this, when you could... be there. In the rain or the sunset or anywhere you want to be. So....

"So Great-Pop...."

All at once her sobs stilled. The pressure and the pain in her chest were still there, the tears pricked behind her eyes; she had to sniff hard to breathe through her warm nose, but the sobbing just stopped and she said, in a clear and firm voice, "You can let go now, if you want."

She took the rook she'd pulled down from the closet and she put it in his hand and closed his fingers over it. The carved "I love you" showed from beneath his hand.

Autumn closed her eyes so tightly she saw purple and blue spots. She put all her thoughts in the throne room where she was Princess Reina. She thought about Rook and Toren and Red-Eye and the rain and the hundreds of gold-dust citizens that were figments of their combined imaginations. She imagined the dress she would wear. Maroon—Great-Pop's very favorite color. Maroon with delicate silver embroidery! A thousand little rosebuds all over the bodice and the skirt and the lacy sleeves. And then she was there, standing in silver shoes and a fantastic, tall crown that glinted in the gray-white light of the rain outside the window.

Her hair was braided with beautiful things: baby's breath and flowers and vines and jeweled pins and ribbons of delicate silk, with glitter sprinkled all over it. It was so laden with objects, in fact, that she had to carry her braid in her arms to keep it from pulling her head back.

She could see the marble floor under her feet, polished, her streaked reflection following her as she hurried for the dining hall. She could smell dinner. Something amazing—braised meat and buttery vegetables and champagne. It was going to be a feast! And when she burst through the closed doorway, indeed, there was a feast laid out on the table, a feast to feed a hundred people. Except it was only Rook and Toren, standing together near the window. She saw the glittery gold trail of a servant disappearing out of the room. The two stood close— closer than she could ever remember seeing them, and Rook's arm was around Toren's waist.

She watched, biting her lip for a moment, before she ran to them, arms still full of her hair.

"Great-Pop," she whispered as she approached him, and as Toren turned to her, he smiled, genuinely surprised to see her. She looked him full in the face and dropped her braid so sparkling sapphires showered from her hair and clattered against the floor. She could barely control herself as she cried, "Tom Johnson! That's your name, Great-Pop. Tommy Johnson!"

His face became literature, and she could read all the amazing memories that had—in that moment of speaking his name—returned to him. He blinked dark eyes at her and reached out with trembling hands and touched her heart-shaped face and pulled her to him in the mightiest hug.

"Autumn," he breathed, "Autumn, you're here! Why are you here?"

"I'm just here to make sure you found your way, Great-Pop. And to say good-bye," she said through her tears, leaning back to look at him. "I just wanted to tell you good-bye."

He didn't understand her words at first, and then she nodded over to Rook, and she called him by his real name, clear and true. "Hello, Roy." And when Great-Pop turned and saw Roy standing there as young and healthy as he had been when they were both alive together, his whole face cracked, and he began to cry. He knuckled at his eyes, the tears spilling over.

"Roy?" he breathed, shaking his head. His mouth had come open, and for a moment, there were no more words. And then, it burst from him, "My God, Roy? Roy? Is that really you?"

She thought she could sneak quietly out of the palace and leave them alone to their reunion and their Forever. But as she turned on her slipper-heels, she felt two pairs of warm, heavy arms around her, hugging her tightly, lifting her up off the ground, and for a long moment, she just let herself be hugged. She felt their arms. She memorized the embrace.

"Thank you," Roy whispered into her ear. "Thank you, so much, Autumn."

"Autumn?" Great-Pop asked against her cheek. She could feel wetness and didn't know if it was his tears or hers. "Autumn, can you please do me a favor?"

She nodded silently, turned away from them both, feet dangling, but clinging to their arms. She didn't want to go back, but she knew she had to. This place wasn't for her. It wasn't her time. But she wanted to see the Sunset Forest one last time, and so she imagined it, and when she blinked, they were all there together. The radiant golden light shone on her face and cast long shadows behind them.

"Autumn. You have to tell Virginia about this place," Great-Pop said, and she cut her eyes, a little uncertainly, up at Roy. She was surprised by the warm expression on his face.

"You do," Roy agreed. "Tell her how to find us. Tell her to come visit when she's ready."

"I will," Autumn promised. Then she closed her eyes on the cottage, and when she opened them, she was back in the bedroom with Great-Pop, holding his quiet body. His chest silently rose and fell, but she peeled back her arms and slipped off the bed, having done what she needed to do.

When Aunt Amy Jo called Mama later that night to tell her that Great-Pop had slipped away from them, Autumn was not surprised, and her sadness was mixed with comfort. Autumn put her arms around her mother and held her while she cried openly at the loss they shared.

Chapter 36

"Roy, what *is* this place?"

Tommy couldn't keep his hands off of anything. He gently touched the fence and the flowers and ran his palms over the stones that made up the cottage. He wandered, as a stranger, into every room, crushing the sheets on the beds in his hands and knocking knuckles against the pots and pans that hung over the small stove. He streaked the windowpanes with his fingerprints and rustled the curtains, and many, many times, he stopped his exploration, and Tommy reached out and touched Roy himself. His shoulder or his cheek or his lips or his eyelids. He traced the outer edge of his ears. He ran his hands down Roy's arms. He held Roy close, pushed him away to look at him, and then smothered him in another desperate hug. And then he was off, outside again in the garden, putting his hands on the frayed rope of the swing, splashing in the well water he drew up in the bucket, bending and running his fingers through the sweet-smelling grass, feeling and experiencing it all. Everything about the place pleased him. Every inch of the land was perfect and peaceful.

"I promised you," Roy reminded him. "I promised you that I was going to find a place where we could be together forever."

"You went all out," Tommy teased, plucking a wildflower and twirling the stem in his fingers. And then without warning he grabbed Roy's hand and pulled him down to the ground. Roy went willingly, and they sat together, knees to knees. Roy moved so close to Tommy that he was almost on top of him, and he kissed him. "Everything feels like a blur."

"It'll clear," Roy promised against his lips. He took his time with the kiss, savored it, savored Tommy. "It'll clear, and you'll remember everything. And it won't hurt. It'll just be."

Tommy whispered, "I've missed you so, so much. There wasn't a day, Roy, that I didn't think of you. I love you."

"I know you do," Roy said, with a gentle and contented smile. "But it's *good* to hear it again, Tommy Johnson. I love you too. I've been watching you every minute since I woke up here. Watching and waiting."

Tommy chuckled. "I hope I did you proud."

"You did me more than proud. Look at that fiery little great-granddaughter of yours."

"She's something else."

"She's *you*," Roy said proudly. "She's got your spirit. You passed on your spirit, and it's in Autumn." And then with a grin he said, "I have so much to show you, Tommy. Every inch of this land I created myself. This valley goes so much farther than the cottage and the woods and castle. We can start exploring any time you want. See what I've done. Add to it yourself. *Anything* you want; you've got creative rights. This is *our* home now."

"I want to see it," Tommy breathed. "I want to see *everything*. But first, wasn't there… something about a prize?" he asked, and they collapsed back into the cool grass, laughing, loving.

CHAPTER 37

MAMA FIXED Autumn's hair on the day of Great-Pop's funeral. She took her time, combing it all out and then twisting it into one long braid that fell against her back. Mama looked pretty, even in all black, even with her shining eyes and her pink-tipped nose. Autumn wore black too, because it was expected. But she didn't think that was what Great-Pop would have wanted. He would have wanted everyone to be comfortable. He would have loved it if she showed up to his funeral in her tiara. But at twelve, Autumn had started to realize that funerals were more for the living than for the dead.

Before the service, Autumn sat on her bed and laid out all the pictures of Great-Pop that she'd found in their photo albums. There weren't that many—but what would have been enough, really? Her favorite was the one with Great-Pop and the dachshunds. He was standing on the porch, looking off to the right, talking with someone, and Rudy and Oscar stared right at the camera, one on either side of him. His sentinels.

"Great-Pop," she whispered, running her fingertips over Rudy's wire-haired muzzle and Oscar's short-haired black and tan head, "let's just talk for a while."

She rearranged her photos, choosing her favorites, ordering them oldest—the black-and-white one of Tommy and Roy—to most recent—Great-Pop and Great-Mom smiling together at Christmas.

She thought about when she was six years old, and she'd followed him on his walk through the park. She was being sneaky, just like he was the day he first talked to Roy. And just like Roy had known that day, Great-Pop knew she was there all along. He caught her when he stopped suddenly, and she barreled right into the back of him.

"Why Autumn, I didn't know you were out here." And he winked at her, which meant that he really did. "Want to walk with me for a while?"

"Tell me a story, Great-Pop!" she said. The tiny red rocks that made up the walking trail crunched under her feet. "I love your stories!"

"You do?" he asked with a grin.

"I want you to tell me every story ever. Every one you know!"

"Every story, huh?"

"As long as they have to do with you."

"But then, Autumn, you'd know all my secrets."

"I want to know your secrets!" she insisted warmly, swinging his hand as she walked. Some teenagers were playing basketball on the court, and she watched them as they passed.

"I'm just an old man with nothing to tell."

"That's not true, Great-Pop," she said brightly, hopping over the crack where the gravel became concrete. "You're my very favorite in the whole wide world."

In her room, Autumn smiled and kissed a picture before laying it back down. "You're still my favorite, Great-Pop."

Jack picked them up in his old truck. He nodded at her, and she nodded back, noticing out of the corner of her eye the way he took Mama's hand and silently squeezed it. She couldn't ever remember Daddy holding Mama's hand.

The funeral home was crowded and hot. They couldn't even all fit into the main chapel, and there were several large groups that had to sit in the spillover areas, watching the preacher speak on a closed-circuit television. People who had known Great-Pop fifty years ago and more showed up. Friends from long ago. There were so many kids and grandkids that she and Mama and Jack were pretty far back. But that didn't matter either.

Aunt Vivian gave the eulogy, which surprised Autumn. If she still needed that mystery apology from Great-Pop, she'd put it aside for today at least. When she spoke about her father, it was about his kindness and his generosity and how much he meant to everyone who met him. The tears that rolled down her cheeks were tears of pride at his accomplishments, tears of sadness for her family's loss, but not tears of anger.

In the end, Autumn walked past his open casket and put the white rose the funeral director handed her onto his chest. She was one of the very last to lay her rose. Great-Pop had so much family—there were so many roses. He was covered in them, a blanket of white blooms. She didn't say good-bye then. She didn't need to.

Many people came up to Mama after the service and told her what a good man her grandfather was. Autumn listened to them and beamed inside. He *was* a good man, and he'd touched a lot of hearts. Even Hannah, who looked like she was going to die of boredom while she texted from the corner of the chapel, couldn't dampen the day or lessen the impact of all those warm words.

As they waited for the cars that would take them to the gravesite, Autumn happened to look up and see a very old woman standing in the doorway. Her breath caught in her throat. She didn't know why she recognized her, except that she looked like Great-Pop—even in her old age. She stumble-walked, hunched, down the aisle. Her short silver hair was lovingly curled and sprayed by younger hands. A woman helped her along, summer-tanned and pretty. They moved slowly, arm in arm. Autumn's feet carried her away from her mother's side and she crept nearer to the pair. She must have been sitting in the back or the spillover room, or maybe she'd missed the service altogether. But she was here now.

"Excuse me?" Autumn asked politely. The old woman turned her face to Autumn, but her eyes were hazy and sightless.

"Grandma," the young woman said, patting her arm, "there's a pretty little redhead speaking to you."

"Oh!" she said in a croaking voice. Her smile was wide. She was missing teeth. "Hello, dear. What's your name?"

"Autumn," she said, and with the pain of expectation, she asked, "Is your name Ardeth?"

"You know me?" the woman asked, shock pulling her wrinkled face into a contorted mask.

"You came." Autumn, who had held tears at bay through the whole service, now swiped at her eyes indelicately with her dress sleeve.

"You know me," she said again. "Tommy told you about me?"

"No," she laughed, sniffing hard. "No, but Roy did."

"How is that even possible?" Ardeth asked.

"C'mon," Autumn insisted, instead of explaining, "you really need to meet my Great-Mom. She will be so pleased to know you."

The clouds that had been threatening rain all day opened up and poured at the gravesite, and she watched the sky instead of the casket as it was lowered into the ground. All around her, family and friends and acquaintances who had been touched by Great-Pop sniffled and stifled their sobs. She took that moment to think about Great-Pop and Roy and how they were happy together. Ardeth was sitting up front right next to Great-Mom. Autumn was glad she had come. She knew Great-Pop would have been so pleased to see his favorite sister after all this time. She thought about Roy and Tommy, and she hoped they could see this gathering from the valley.

That evening, after the meal, when many of her family members had packed up their things and gone home, and there were only about twelve of them left at the house, Great-Mom announced that she was going to lie down for a little while. She insisted they stay, if they wanted, and eat more and talk and be together. No one followed her.

Except Autumn.

She padded silently along behind Great-Mom until they were at the door of the master bedroom, and then Autumn made a little noise so she wouldn't scare her.

"Oh, Autumn," she said, and her voice was heavy with exhaustion. "I'm sorry, sweetheart. I need to lie down."

"I understand. I just wondered if you wanted me to tell you a story while you were going to sleep."

In her purse in the living room was a long note—longer than any note she had ever written to Emma—longer than any journal entry or school writing project. It was the longest thing she had ever put to paper. Details of the Sunset Valley and the Rain Kingdom. Great-Pop and Roy had asked her to tell Great-Mom how to get there, but she didn't really understand it herself. She thought that maybe it was heaven. A special slice of it, reserved just for them and the people they cared most for. She thought that if she could give Great-Mom a really excellent description of the things she had seen there, then she would know what she was looking for when it was her time. She would give it to her tomorrow maybe.

"A story?" Great-Mom asked, shuffling across the carpet. She walked behind her changing screen and slowly put on her nightgown while Autumn looked at the things she kept on her dresser. Pearls and perfume and gold-handled brushes—everything an elegant woman needed.

"It's about Great-Pop."

She heard her great-grandmother draw in a long, sad breath.

"Please don't cry, Great-Mom. He's happy now. I just know it. He's with Roy."

Great-Mom moved slowly from around the screen. Her hair, which she always kept so tightly knotted, was now a snowy drift around her face. She couldn't have looked more surprised if Tommy himself were standing before her.

"He... told you?" she whispered, her voice quavering under the weight of it.

"Yes. Yes. He told me all about Roy."

Very slowly, Great-Mom moved to her bed and sat down on the mattress. She was so light that it hardly seemed to give under her weight. Rudy and Oscar—who had been staying with Aunt Terri— were back at home, and the two dachshunds lay together on Great-Pop's side of the bed.

"How much did he tell you?"

"A lot," Autumn said, knowing there were many, many stories she had not been able to hear. Maybe one day, when they were all together in the valley, she could hear the rest. "Do you want me to tell you one?"

"Will you?" Great-Mom laughed, just a little, through her tears, like a giddy little girl, like Autumn had laughed the first time Great-Pop offered her this special part of his life. "Will you please tell me about him?"

"I'll tell you everything!" Autumn insisted, her cheeks flushing.

Great-Mom patted the side of the bed, and Autumn quickly kicked off her shoes and climbed up beside her. She steeled herself, trying to think where to start. But of course! She would start at the beginning, and she would do her very, very best not to leave out a single detail.

"Great-Pop first noticed Roy one day in church...."

RAINE O'TIERNEY is an always-writing, boundlessly enthusiastic, exclamation point addict! (!!!) She is known for declaring every day "the best day EVER!" and everything her "all-time FAVORITE!" Despite this (obnoxious?) exuberance, she still somehow manages to have a wonderfully encouraging husband (who also writes M/M rom!) and an amazing group of friends and colleagues who continue to support (read: put up with) her. Raine spends her days working as a library lady, fighting the good fight for intellectual freedom.

Raine tumbled headlong into the world of M/M romance after discovering yaoi back in 2004. A new passion was immediately born and her writing life became dedicated to men who love men! Raine frequently changes genres, but she always tries to imbue her stories with what she calls "The Sweetness" of which there are five Fs (first loves, first times, fidelity, forever-type endings, and… friskiness?).

After twenty-plus years of writing and dreaming, a decade spent working on M/M, and a year of being a lionheart, Raine is so pleased to join the Dreamspinner Press family!

Contact her through any of the channels below to discuss writing, point-and-click adventure games, and which kinds of dachshunds are the best kinds of dachshunds!

E-mail: Raineotierney@gmail.com

Website: http://raineotierney.com/

Facebook: https://www.facebook.com/RaineOTierneyAuthor

Twitter: https://twitter.com/RaineOTierney

Hearts in Reverie:

Sweet Giordan, Please Remember

Raine O'Tierney

http://www.dreamspinnerpress.com

TRUSTING LOVE

Mari Evans

http://www.dreamspinnerpress.com

MICHAEL MURPHY

SWAN
SONG
FOR AN
UGLY
DUCKLING

http://www.dreamspinnerpress.com

Shiny!

AMY LANE

http://www.dreamspinnerpress.com

Michael
Rupured

HAPPY
Independence
DAY

http://www.dreamspinnerpress.com

HUSBAND HUNTERS

RICK R. REED

www.ingramcontent.com/pod-product-compliance
Lightning Source LLC
Chambersburg PA
CBHW060100260626
47160CB00005B/1736